The C

Geoffrey Beattie is an ac............ ist and broadcaster. Born in Belfast, he obtained a First in Psychology from the University of Birmingham and a Ph.D. from Trinity College, Cambridge.

He is now Professor of Psychology at Manchester University. He was awarded the prestigious Spearman Medal by the British Psychological Society for 'published psychological work of outstanding merit'. In addition, he has written regularly for the *Guardian* and the *Independent* and has published several books on aspects of contemporary British life. His book, *On the Ropes: Boxing as a Way of Life*, was shortlisted for the William Hill Sports Book of the Year Award. His latest book, *Head to Head: Uncovering the Psychology of Sporting Success* is available as a Victor Gollancz Paperback Original. *The Corner Boys* is his first novel.

GEOFFREY BEATTIE

The Corner Boys

INDIGO

First published in Great Britain 1998
by Victor Gollancz

This Indigo edition published 1999
Indigo is an imprint of the Cassell Group
Wellington House, 125 Strand, London WC2R 0BB

A catalogue record for this book is
available from the British Library.

ISBN 0 575 40194 X

Printed and bound in Great Britain by
Guernsey Press Co. Ltd, Guernsey, Channel Isles

2 4 6 8 9 7 5 3 1

This book is dedicated to Zoe, Ben and Sam, who never needed life on the corner

REMEMBER 1690

Wall Graffito in Belfast

**RE-MEMBERING
(BECOMING MEMBERS AGAIN)**

Edwards, Potter and Middleton, *The Psychologist*, 1992

When I am dead
Cry for me a little
Think of me sometimes
But not too much.
Think of me now and again
As I was in life
At some moments it's pleasant to recall
But not for long.
Leave me in peace
And I shall leave you in peace
And while you live
Let your thoughts be with the living.

Indian Prayer
(traditional)

1

I found the trainers below the bed, eventually, after a good deal of looking. They were dirty. I don't mean that they weren't white, or that they weren't pristine, or that they were stained with sweat, I mean that they were caked with mud. Fucking caked with hard baked mud. They weren't the real thing anyway – they weren't Nike Airs or Reebok or anything like that, my mother got them for me cheap from somebody at work, so it shouldn't have been that important what state they were in, but it was. It was a big night out for me.

I didn't normally wear my trainers to go out in at nights. I preferred my boots. One of my mates got me those, in the right size as well. They were the genuine article with that famous sole. I can't remember what it's called, but it's like walking on air. That's what they say anyway. When I say that he got them for me, I mean that he lifted them for me. He nicked them and gave them to me. Or rather they were on permanent loan to me. He might ask for them back one day, if we ever fell out. But I didn't think there was much chance of that. Me and my mates never fell out. We had arguments, but we never fell out. You can't fall out with your mates. Who would you go to if you were in trouble if you did?

But I couldn't wear my boots that night, even though they were the real thing, and the trainers were some make that neither my mates nor I had ever heard of. I wanted to look a bit laid-back, a bit cool. Or coolish. Different anyway.

I was wearing a loose vest, loose cotton jeans and hopefully the trainers, if I could clean them up a bit. Not the boots. It was hard not to wear them. But the boots wouldn't have looked right with gear like that. I'd never worn a vest like that before, something loose, just sort of hanging there. We all wore tight clothes, not deliberately, that was just the style me and my mates liked. That was just us. Tight little swathed bundles that might just snap open at any moment. That's what I thought sometimes, when I was bored or distracted, and I could just stand back and look at us all standing there at the corner, just hanging about.

I had put a red bulb in the threadbare socket dangling down in my bedroom the previous night. It helped. It made the bedroom with the damp walls look warm, you couldn't see the damp patches any longer or the long zigzagging crack in the plaster which started at the socket and finished near the windowframe. I stood in front of the mirror on the dressing table looking at myself in this warm pink glow, imagining how others might see me in this new gear. Others who didn't know me.

I'd been invited to a party, up on the hill by a girl who knew me from church. A wee quiet girl I used to know from Sunday school who had a long dark fringe, and big greyish-blue nervous-looking eyes. She looked permanently frightened. I bumped into her on the bus into town. She invited me to her party. The funny thing was that I wasn't at all sure that she had actually intended to ask me to her party. She just sort of came out with it because I had sat down beside her on the bus. I wouldn't have even sat beside her if there had been any other seats, but there weren't. She hadn't noticed that. She was too nervous to look around her on the bus, the way you do. She thought she had to talk to me because I had chosen the seat beside her, even though there wasn't much actual choosing involved in it. Obviously the party was on her mind, and because she was nervous she

12

talked about it, and then asked me to come along. On my own. She made me laugh because she kept stressing that. 'Come on your own,' she said. She said it twice, as if I might bring my big dog with me or a big gang of fucking hoods. I was pleased to be asked though.

But I didn't want to turn up in my boots and my denims. Her friends wouldn't be like that, her friends wouldn't be from around our neighbourhood. Some of the lads who liked rap tried calling it 'the hood' but that just made me laugh. We weren't the boys from the hood, we were just the boys from the corner. Anyway, her friends wouldn't be from the hood or the corner, she was far too quiet for the lads around our way. I knew that. I wanted to try out a new style. That was the problem with our street, you couldn't really change how you looked. We all dressed the same, more or less. We all dressed in a practical sort of way, you might say. Your arse would be out of your trousers in no time, if you wore thin cotton pants around here. My style for getting over yard walls in a hurry was to swivel on my arse. That was just my personal style. A lot of my mates did it differently. They threw their leg over, I just sort of spun on my arse. I got over fences in the same sort of way, whenever we were out in the country that is, but it was mainly yard walls we had to deal with. We had to get over a lot of them in a hurry. I needed good hard-wearing jeans for all of this climbing and scrambling about, not cool fucking caks with a big hole in the arse.

I held the trainers right under the light to see them better. That was the problem with a red bulb, it made everything look good, but it just wasn't very bright. I'd thrown the other bulb that had been in the socket over the yard wall to hear it pop. It sounded like a man with no teeth smacking his lips, it made a quiet sad little popping noise. One of my mates had egged me on to do this. He told me about the noise that bulbs made when they exploded. That was his word, 'explode'. 'Where have you been living?' I said when I saw him again. 'Not fucking Belfast by the sound of things. Some explosion that.' But he said it was just a figure of speech, and not that important.

I should have held on to the other bulb, then I might have been able to see the trainers properly. I could see the grass sticking out of the soles like long thick whiskers. I knew the trainers were brown, but that was more a deduction than anything else. I had played football in them a few days before. You can't really see brown, when you've got a red light. I thought to myself that I could wash them and wear them wet, or just leave them as they were. But I didn't want to squelch my way into the party, and draw attention to myself. So I came downstairs with the vest on and the trainers with clumps of mud and grass sticking out from under them, leaving a grassy trail down the stairs for my mother to clear up later.

My mother was sitting with one of her friends in front of the fire in the front room. They were having a wee smoke and a wee drink. The fumes from the drink and their cheap perfume and all that smoke were locked into our front room. I coughed as I came through the door, as if I was commenting on what they were doing, and fanned the smoke away with my hand. It was almost a nervous affliction on my part, every time I smelt smoke I started making little fanning movements from the wrist. Little sharp wristy movements. This type of gesture always irritated my mother. I don't know why.

'Smoke never did anybody any harm,' she would say. 'My mother and father both smoked all their life and I'm healthy.' This was true, but only up to a point. There was a lot of heart disease up our way, most of it undiagnosed. That's how people died up our way and it was just accepted. It was almost as if angina wasn't really anything to do with being unhealthy. A bad ticker was just what you got when you got to a certain age. It was a sign of maturity.

It was probably the perfume that made me cough anyway. I always thought it was funny the way women dressed up for each other just to sit in each other's houses having a wee drink and a wee smoke. They called this a big night out. It was always a wee drink and a wee smoke, by the way, never a big one. I always thought this might have something to do with Protestant guilt. A wee drink wasn't as bad somehow. I wondered if Taigs called it 'a wee drink' as well. I didn't know the answer to that one. I didn't know any Taigs well enough to ask them.

She pointed at my vest, showing a lot of bare neck, and asked me where I was going dressed like that on a dark October night. I told her that I was going out.

'Out where?' she asked.

'Just out,' I said.

Her friend laughed. 'Couldn't you be a wee bit more specific than that for your mother?' she said. 'She worries about you out on your own with all the killing that goes on in this wee town of ours.'

But I was never out on my own, she should have known that.

'Yeah OK then,' I said. 'I'm going out and about.'

The friend laughed again. 'He takes after you,' she said. 'You were like that when you were his age. You were a cheeky wee shite too.'

'Couldn't you be a bit more sensible for once,' my mother said. 'Put a coat on or you'll catch the death of cold.'

I stood there looking out at the rain, realizing that I had no coat that would go with what I was wearing. My leather bomber jacket wouldn't look right, neither would my old school blazer with the gold crown on the pocket. I had no coat that fitted, so I had no coat to wear. So I said that I was just going down the street to see a mate, and I set off running into the October night, and down towards the corner.

They were all there already. In retrospect, I don't know how I thought that I was going to just slip past them. They were standing in a long line in the wet drizzle, soaked to the skin having a laugh about something or other. 'Look at trendy baaaalicks there,' they said as I walked towards them. They knew that I hadn't come to stand at the corner dressed like that, they knew that I was off out somewhere. They all knew I was up to something. I could tell by their eyes. It was always more difficult to lie to them than to my mother. Don't ask me why. They got it out of me in no time. I confessed about the party up the hill. So they took a vote, and the vote was for us all to go to the party, so we all set off together up the hill to the party, me with no coat on, with the damp October rain, which sticks to you, flattening my carefully brushed hair.

We walked slowly past the houses with the sundials and the rose bushes, with little yapping dogs peeking out behind thick brown velvet curtains in long pink lounges. We didn't have velvet curtains or a pink lounge, or a little yapping dog, or a sundial, or even a garden for that matter. Well that's not strictly true, our next-door neighbour had a sundial in her yard. Her son got it for her, probably from up this selfsame street, an oasis of lower-middle class calm and aspiration, built on a hill above the flatter, greyer streets of North Belfast. You could see Belfast Lough from up there and what was left of the shipyard, and on a good day when you looked beyond the lough you could see the hills of Scotland in the distance.

We turned up at the party together, the way mates do. I knocked on the door, and the rest of the lads hung back waiting for me to sort everything out for them. But it was no good, they wouldn't let us in. It was as simple as that. It wasn't me and a few mates out there, it was a gang that had turned up. The door was kept locked.

The girl who I vaguely knew came to the window and

mouthed that she was sorry but the party was full. That's what she said 'full'. I could see all these little heads behind the curtains darting about this way and that. They reminded me of tadpoles. The last time I saw any tadpoles they were on our kitchen floor in the old days before the Housing Executive did our house up. I had a pish in an empty milk-bottle that had some tadpoles in it. I didn't remember that I'd put them there, until I felt the warm water touch the end of my dick which I was holding into the end of the bottle. I couldn't be bothered going to the toilet outside, you see, so I just picked up this bottle in the kitchen, and filled it – well more than filled it, because it was half-full already with the tadpoles. The tadpoles and the pish ended up all over the floor. It took me a few seconds to realize what was happening, and by then it was too late. The tadpoles were swimming for their lives across our floor in a frothy yellow sea.

We stood out on her drive in the rain looking at each other. At least my mates were dressed right. I shivered in my vest and my muddy brown trainers. We walked back home and then walked down by the side of the old Victorian graveyard, and a few of the lads clambered in. I knew they'd dive in. There were tombs in there, and it was easy to get into them. We'd all been in there before and messed about a wee bit. But I didn't go in that night, I said that I wasn't dressed properly for shinning up walls.

When they came back out, one of them had something up his jacket. I could tell by his grin he had got something good. He made ghosty noises all the way home, and shook his jacket every now and then. It fell out at the bottom of our street. It was a man's skull with some moss growing out of it, or it could have been a woman's because it was so small. But the men were smaller in those days, so it probably belonged to a small rich man, who could afford a substantial final resting place amongst all that Victorian splendour, where he would never be disturbed. Until now, that is. The skull fell on to the pavement at the bottom of our street, and the jaw fell off. We called the wee rich man's head Archie. My mates got bored with it after a while, and left it lying in the street outside my house. I took it in with me and hid it below the bed in a shoebox for the night. I took both bits back to the graveyard the next day, and chucked them over the graveyard wall. At least the skull was back on hallowed ground, even if it was in bits.

So that was the night of the party and my big night out. I didn't even get a wee drink. After that everything was back to normal, back to my little routine.

2

I liked to be out of the house by five at the very latest, before my mother got back. If I didn't, there would be an argument. Her slaving away in that factory, and me sitting on my arse watching television. The television that didn't work properly.

She worked in a thread factory, as an inspector. That was her official title. Mind you I only had her word for that. It sounded like a grand title.

She had to check that the thread, which came down from great oiled rollers near the dusty ceiling, didn't have too many knots in it. Then she checked the thread for oilstains. Finally, she packed the coiled strands away in little brown speckled boxes, which she assembled herself by slotting sharp corners and long cutting flaps into ready-made slits. Twelve of the cones in the one box, all the same colour.

She liked the rows of blue cones the best, the dark blue cones all pointing out in neat rows and columns with no knots or stains. They were a lovely colour of blue, a really deep colour like the blue on a new flag or the blue of the sea at the end of summer, in a holiday brochure. Not the grey sea around here with its ripped and torn seaweed, the dirty green of the seaweed seeping out into the salty water. It was the proper blue, the true blue.

These blues were done late in her shift, before the house-wives' shift came on at five o'clock. These blues were always the last colour of thread to be done. Ernie, the foreman, fixed that.

She didn't just work in a factory, she did three jobs there really. That's what she said. That's what she called them as well. Three jobs, not three small components of one job, nor three small steps in one semi-skilled action, but three separate jobs, each one demanding in itself. Each one required certain attributes. You needed quick hands to put the boxes together and a very quick mind to check for knots and flaws. Oilstains on thread could be difficult to detect in a room like that which wasn't very well lit, and knots were impossible sometimes. But she could do all of this and more in a room with one fluorescent strip out, and the other which flickered away in the corner. 'It could give you a fit that light,' she said. But not her.

'I've never had a fit, never in my whole life,' she would say. 'And I sit at a table like the managers themselves up in their offices above the shop floor. I sit on the very same chairs that they use themselves, when they've done with them. The stuffing might have gone a bit, but they're still good chairs. The girls who work the machines have to stand all day in the same place. On their feet for eight, sometimes ten hours when they fancy a bit of overtime.'

The way she talked about the job you could tell that she regarded herself as a cut above the rest. They only had to do one job. Most of them had just got quick hands. She liked to remind me of that, whenever I told her what somebody in the street had said to me. She'd say, 'Don't listen to them, they only work a machine up in the mill. What do they know?' But they earned more than her for working the machines that never stopped during the shift. 'But that work's relentless,' she always said. 'It would make your mind go numb.'

She also collected the Christmas Club money, not only for what used to be the carding room, but the store room next door as well. You needed to be good with figures for that position, and to be trustworthy. Beyond reproach. You don't let just anybody look after the mill's Christmas Club money. This was started in early August, so that half the year was spent looking forward to a few damp days in December. The snow never seems to make it to Belfast, it's the Irish Sea that stops it. That's what our teacher always used to say. 'The Irish Sea is a natural barrier.'

There was the Christmas Club in the baker's for the cakes for Christmas, the butcher's Christmas Club for the turkey, but the mill's Christmas Club was the most important. It was the money you saved for all the rest, the presents for the wee ones. The wee innocent ones who had to have something to look forward to in this part of North Belfast with its bullets and its bombs and its job prospects, which were nil.

For month after month, she kept the money below the bed in the front room in an old shoebox, with all the figures recorded in thick pencil on ripped-out sheets of a short-hand notebook. The cover of the notebook said *Chapmans. Stationer to the Nation.* She had figures running up and down the inside of the cover, the totals underlined. The notebook came from the director of the thread factory's office. It was his little contribution to the well-being of his staff.

'People like to call us millies,' she liked to say, 'but we're not millies any longer. That's the old name. It's not a flax mill any more so how can we be wee millies, wee Belfast millies, we're machine operatives or inspectors. That's our proper titles. People in Belfast used to talk about millies as if we were good things, easy touches, but you can't talk about machine operatives like that, or inspectors. It doesn't sound the same. They can't put you down the same way the way they used to when we worked in the spinning mill. They'd like to, but they can't.'

She had started in that flax mill when she was fifteen, and she had worked her way up to be an inspector in a thread factory at forty-five. That was good progress, even if her title was hotly contested on our street. Old Lizzie from next door said that she wasn't really an 'inspector' as such, she just inspected the thread, and that was different. You had to do more than inspect the thread to be an inspector. There was a proper inspector who was in charge and he had an office all of his own up with the rest of the managers. My mother told her she should mind her own business, and that she was doing his work so she was really the inspector. He was just an idle man with a fancy title.

At least she was trying to make something of herself. That was always the source of the torrent that swept us along night after night. She seemed to believe that we were all made of clay waiting to be sculpted. Earth to be shaped by our own hands. Our own quick hands. But some were just dirt. You could tell who they were. It was hard enough getting by where we lived without mixing with dirt.

She had been making something of herself since she just turned fifteen, and before that when she used to sit at the front in the class so that the teacher could send her for his messages. He used to let her answer the phone at school and send her to the library to choose his six books, which she would then carry carefully back for him. She was clever, and she knew his taste in reading. He trusted her. He told me about this, when I was sitting in the same place a generation on. But two rows back. I was never sent to the library. I was smart, but I wasn't like her.

I was allowed to answer the telephone once. The telephone was kept in a cabinet with some mercury for experiments, the next shelf down from the mercury. The phone rang loudly and he called my name and told me to pick it up. It had got round to being my turn. It was the girls' turn first, and then the boys'. Boys with any obvious mental disability were left to last. The class watched me move slowly to the mercury cupboard. I picked it up, it was a woman's voice. She sounded like another schoolteacher in some chalky room, in a thick brown tweed skirt. I forgot to leave the telephone to the side when I went to get him. I put it right back on the bit in the middle. I wasn't used to telephones, we didn't have one in our house. So I wasn't allowed to touch the phone after that.

I was still just clay. That's what I would say. I had no blueprints to follow. Not yet anyway.

I had tried to be interested years ago in her line of work. She took me into the mill one dinnertime, and showed me the rollers and the heaped mountains of thread. The air tickled my throat and made me cough. The foreman Ernie smelt of cigarettes and aftershave that he splashed on. It smelt tangy, like lemons that had gone mouldy and therefore smelt even stronger. It hit the back of your throat. I wouldn't have been able to give a name to the aftershave myself, but my mother told me afterwards what he liked. All the girls knew.

'Ernie always smells lovely,' she would say. 'Expensive stuff. Only the best. He uses it as deodorant. He has a little squirt at dinnertime, so that he smells nice in the afternoon.' The aftershave was bought out of the interest on the Christmas Club money. It was his little bonus.

Ernie was a great hit with the girls from the mill. He told them when they could go for a smoke break, and how long they could spend at the toilet. It was important to keep the rollers running at all times, so Ernie had to be on top of things. But he liked a smoke himself, so he would sometimes join the girls at the door at the back of the mill, where he would complain about the price of fags, and they would tell him all about themselves and their relationships. They would talk all about their no-good husbands who wouldn't work, whilst Ernie up in the mill grafted away, keeping the thundering rollers moving, even when he stood out in the back smoking and laughing and listening to all the details of the girls' lives and loves.

You could smell his aftershave from that damp wooden

frame at the back of the mill. The aroma burnt brown rings in the light timber frame. You could tell how many years Ernie had been standing there from the spacing of the rings on the wooden frame, like an old oak with history written into it. Ernie's history was worn deep into the fabric of the building. It wasn't really the aroma, of course, that marked the wood, it was the fumes from his aftershave and his cigarettes. A combination like no other – expensive aftershave used to cover hot damp bodily smells and smoke from a chimney that never stopped bellowing it out.

Ernie had worked his way into the firm and worked his way up nicely until he was indispensable. Now he knew all the ins and outs of the job. He knew where everything was and how much everything cost, and he knew in which order the threads should go through the machines in order to please the girls, to keep them happy. And you have to keep the girls happy. If the blue wasn't kept to the last there would be a riot. The girls looked out for the sweetest of blues, the true blue, that's what they called it, the true blue – that was their favourite. They would recognize the true blue anywhere. It was always the true blue that went through last in the shift, except on a Tuesday when the bluey-green went last. That was the way things were done, and Ernie knew it. Sometimes he'd slip the true blue in early for a wee joke, but they'd all chant and clap and whistle, until he did it right. But Ernie liked keeping all the girls on their toes.

Ernie was a great friend to all the girls. That's how they liked to put it. A great friend, unlike their husbands. And a great comfort in times of distress. These times were frequent in a community like ours without much proper work.

Ernie was a short bald man, with small narrow colourless eyes, and a large fat neck. He would pass our house, but he never really smiled at me. The face he put on was too quick for a genuine smile, these were half-smiles he tossed my way whenever he saw me. His shirt collar was always open, even in winter, and you could see a ring of grime. I thought he was just dirty and that he really did need his aftershave as deodorant. My mother told me that his wife didn't look after him properly.

He always said that I reminded him of my father, but he would add my father was a good-looking man, and a better man than I would ever be.

'If you turn out to be half the man your da was, you'll be a good un,' is what he always said. Sometimes he didn't say the whole thing. Sometimes he'd just say, 'If you turn out to be half the man,' and leave it at that. I knew what he meant, I knew he was talking about my da, up in Roselawn, under that wet clay in a new plot, with space left for my mother and me. But some of the lads that I knocked about with thought he meant that if I turned out to be half a man I'd be doing OK, because I wasn't even that at the moment. That was their little joke. They didn't really think he was saying that.

At least, I don't think so.

My mother would always go misty-eyed when my father was mentioned like this. But I know that Ernie only said this to impress her. He had a soft moist warm handshake. He would hug my mother, and tell me how well she was coping with the loss of her husband in the prime of her life. Then he would go back to the mill with its roaring spindles which seemed to have a life of their own, and functioned perfectly adequately whether Ernie was physically present or not.

When she got home from work and talked about how one of the rollers was causing the thread to come through with too many knots, I would sit there trying to show interest. 'How many knots is too many?' I would enquire. But she always thought I was just trying to be funny at her expense. So I'd normally slip out just before five and go for a wee dander. I would go down to the bookie's, and stand by the door watching the mugs trudge in and out clutching their dockets, or round the park. There wasn't much to choose between them some days. That particular day, it was warm for the golden flux of mid-autumn, so it was the park with the loud *cak cak cak* of crows above empty sharp nests balancing in the long thin branches of the already bare chestnut trees, stripped naked by the wind through the iron railings and the boys with short fat sticks out collecting cheesers. The thin branches standing out against the grey sky, like blue veins running up the back of an old greying hand holding up some thorned prize.

I had a lot of free time. I had time on my hands ever since a warm Tuesday in June, a day with light rain coming in off the hills. I remember the day well. You always remember days like this. They stay with you. I remember the feelings of panic at the time, that distraught distracting feeling. I remember the deep well of nausea inside, the chalkdust in the room which had been worn into the fabric of the place and was just waiting for someone to enter the room to disturb it, to fluff it back up into the air. I remember the smells of the room, dusty and old, like the vestry at church, but with human odour. I remember the crispness of the unmarked pink examination papers. I held them up to my nose and sniffed at them, like a dog finding his way through fresh new meadows. Everything depended on this, on me being able to find my way through it. I sniffed again and again, hoping that it might make a difference. I remember starting to scan another long winding sentence, and then I remember everything stopping for me. The future stopped suddenly with a great shudder inside me and a loud piercing noise from outside. A wail from beyond me that could not be silenced. But this noise could just as well have been coming from inside my very being. It was so loud and so out of control.

There was a bomb scare. The alarm went, louder than any of us remembered from before, when they were as regular as the bluey-green thread last on a Tuesday. Teachers scurried about the place, quick pointless dashes here and there. They had forgotten what to do. Flustered, stammered requests for instructions, loud contradictory orders back. Those superior voices stopping and starting, not finishing, jumping ahead of themselves. It was funny to listen to it all. And watch. The fear in their faces leaking out. Once it had been routine, now they were trying to learn it all over again. I heard one new member of staff ask, 'What exactly is a bomb alert? Is it serious?'

You weren't allowed to run anywhere in this fine school, and here they were running and sliding on the slippy waxed floors, their black gowns exuding wisps of chalkdust, flapping out behind them. Long shiny corridors and tight corners, their long black gowns, worn shiny in parts, getting tangled all around them. If you narrowed your eyes they looked like wet wounded crows, long glinting feathers, crippled staccato movements, going nowhere. They were trying to keep their dignity amongst all that confusing fear of a school with a bomb alert. The fear on their part. The top halves and the bottom halves of their faces at odds with each other. The mouth saying one thing, the eyes telling a completely different story. The face in great segments ripped apart by fear and dread. All those children, all that responsibility. But I knew it wasn't a bomb. Nobody wanted hundreds of mutilated schoolboys and schoolgirls on a wet Tuesday afternoon in June in Belfast. They just didn't.

I knew that.

We were ushered out towards the front of the building, through another room smelling of fear of a different sort. The alarms still deafening. One girl had wet herself. I walked slowly past the puddle on her seat. I saw it for myself, a deep yellow puddle that must have taken some time to fill, in a red plastic chair with a battered rounded seat. I started to walk even slower. I watched it seep through the crack in the seat and drip slowly on to the polished floor. We were in a line. I wanted to put my finger into it, to see how deep it really was. I slowed the whole snaking procession down. I watched the droplets form, linger for a while and then fall. It was such a sight. The polished floors and probity of that school, with something uncontrolled and uncontrollable happening right in the middle of it, with nobody able to do anything about it.

The whole procession got slower and slower, as I played by the rules in my own game. I wasn't going to run for them. One teacher nudged me in the back. He wanted to get out himself. I slowed down even more. We got to the playground and the light June rain. We were told not to talk. We were in the middle of an exam for goodness' sake. It was obvious that we shouldn't talk. We were supposed to just stand there not discussing anything, even the girl with wet knickers who must have felt very cold at this point. I started to think about the exam again. I watched the faces of boys and girls, some scared, some acting scared to make the whole thing more dramatic, throwing looks at each other, not talking. Not breaking school rules, even now, but egging each other into some kind of fear to make the day more memorable.

The school building looked formidable from this angle. I had never stood just below the clock tower with the chance to look up and study its grand, symmetrical Victorian features. You weren't allowed to. There was an invisible chalk mark on the playground which cordoned off this section of the school. Pupils were not permitted inside the mark. I enjoyed standing there. I had been there before, but never like this, with time on my hands, to just stand and look.

Teachers were completing their search. From a distance you could sense their relief. I narrowed my eyes and watched the crows emerge flapping and waving, picking up bags and boxes, extending their long necks, peering inside. My eyes narrowed and almost closed, just ambient light forcing itself through the crack. The crows faded, and words came back, slowly and sequentially at first, and then ordered on pages, bold lettering at the top, paragraphs below. The question before we left in such a hurry.

I couldn't remember the name of that new town near London beginning with the letter S. The town built on a grid pattern so that traffic didn't build up in the city centre. The new town with green corridors around the suburbs to provide a pleasant environment. The town with all the industry designed to be on the outskirts. A town totally unlike Belfast. I opened my eyes. I needed to use my time. I felt this urgency. I don't know why I did it, but I asked Duck. Why I asked him I don't know. He hadn't a clue. He just shrugged his shoulders, too frightened of the school and its regulations to talk.

Mr Marsh caught me. He was standing right behind me so quietly, so sneakily in that wet playground, as if he knew I would use all that confusion to my advantage. As if he knew that my mind wouldn't be distracted by the bomb that never was. He had a habit of doing that, of coming up behind you when you were least expecting it. In the changing room at the rugby fields, before you got a chance to dress, he would be there standing quietly behind you, saying nothing. But I wasn't thinking about him that day. I wasn't on my guard, the way you should be. I had been too busy.

He pulled me out of the crowd, and said that I would be reported for cheating, and that cheating was a most serious offence. He bent down to talk into my face. I could smell his breath coming out around me, encircling me. I could feel his joy at catching me. It was burning right through him. I always knew he had it in for me, right from the very beginning. He sent me home once for wearing socks that were too gaudy. He told me to go home and change them. But I had no socks to change into, they were all drying in front of the fire kept going through the day to dry the house out, so I stayed at home and took the dog out.

I remember those socks. They had black and white diamonds all over them, except for the sole. The sole was just plain black. He noticed them when I was walking up some stairs ahead of him. My trousers must have been too short. We couldn't afford new trousers every year from the shops they made us use, the official school outfitter in Royal Avenue or some other expensive street like that where they double the price just because of where it is. I got trousers every other year. My mother said that boys don't grow as much as some people think. She would take my turn-ups down after a year. My jeans had turn-ups as well, but that was the fashion. We all had turn-ups on our jeans.

He watched me walk right up to the top of the spiral staircase in front of him, and then he called me back down again. His eyes on my feet the whole time. I thought I must have walked in something on the street to make him do that sort of look with his face. I thought I must have walked some shite into his school, and up that fine old spiral staircase. It had a stone floor, it would wash off. What was he getting so excited about? But there was nothing on the sole of my shoe. It was the socks I suppose that made him look like that. And me. Perhaps it was the thought of me ascending that spiral staircase that really threw him. Me climbing up the ladder, so to speak. Anyway, he called me back down and pointed at the socks. 'What in the name of God are you wearing, boy?' he said.

My Aunty Diane had bought the socks for me for Christmas. She loved those socks. She thought they were very unusual. She thought they were something special, which I suppose they were, in a way. They were not, however, plain charcoal or plain grey.

'Home, boy, go home and change your ankle wear, immediately,' he said. He didn't tell me to come back that day, so I didn't. My aunty was always asking me if I was still wearing the socks. I couldn't tell her that I wasn't allowed to wear them any longer. So I pretended to her. I pretended a lot, to be honest.

Then there was my voice. They were always picking on it. I say that they were picking on it, as if my voice wasn't part of me but something quite separate. I suppose really when I think about it it was me that they were picking on. I went to that school with all the speech characteristics of my natural community and Mr Marsh and all the rest of them who had been given some authority by that school hated every word and syllable of that working-class world. He despised every stock phrase I used again and again to give myself time to think between sentences, between clauses, between words if I needed them.

'You don't need to fill time like that, boy, just say what you think,' he'd say. 'Just speak.'

But I couldn't just speak, I couldn't just say the first thing that came into my head. Not in front of him. I just couldn't. I needed to check what I was going to say. I needed to be careful. I needed to be on my guard.

When I spoke, his look said it all. He didn't need to fill the space between words. His look was eloquent enough. It put me in my place. The boy from the loyalist ghetto, who turned up at the school Christmas disco with his friends from the corner, the friends who shouldn't have been allowed anywhere near the freshly cleaned ancient sandstone of that venerable institution. The corner boy who sneaked into his posh school on a scholarship, the corner boy who should never have been there.

I had my hair cut very short, and he called me the 'shaveling'. I didn't know the word. He knew that I didn't know it.

'Joyce, boy,' he said. 'Joyce.' Or it could have been 'Just, boy, just,' until he said it all again a few days later, enjoying

31

his little joke. My scholarship was thin, on a knife edge. He knew that as well. I learnt the course material. We didn't have Joyce at home, or anybody else for that matter. Joyce wasn't on the course, so I didn't know anything about him or his fancy language. I looked up 'shaveling', and Joyce when I got home in my books. They were there all right. '*Derogatory* a priest or clergyman with a shaved head. A young fellow, youth.' He might have been insulting me, it was hard to tell. Dictionaries never give you the whole story. It depends on how he meant it. I couldn't be sure exactly which meaning he was implying. It's hard trying to learn language from a dictionary. It's like learning a foreign language. You can only get so good at it, in the end.

He told me that if I got my hair cut like that again he would send me home until it grew. I should have a proper schoolboy's haircut, and not one like somebody from the criminal classes. As if only certain classes produce criminals. I thought they were to be found in every walk of life myself.

The alarms stopped. Somebody blew a whistle and some boys cheered. A couple of girls ran off to the toilet. I couldn't face going back to that superior look, so I just headed home. I just felt my feet moving towards the school gate. It was as if I was no longer in control. I kept thinking to myself, I'll stop in a minute, but I never did. I was quite surprised. I was moving away from the school. I was walking up past the rugby ground and the gardens with their sweeping lawns and fancy floral displays. Then up past the houses with the front parlours and porcelain ornaments in the front windows. Porcelain chimney sweeps with a ready smile, covered in ceramic soot, resting after a hard day up some rich person's chimney. Beautiful white teeth shining through all that blackness. Then way up past the church hemmed in by tidy streets. Then round the big bend in the road and up towards the boarded-up shops, with UVF and UFF on the gable walls, and barbed wire on the backs of the entry walls,

32

and the burnt-out bus in front of the park, left there for weeks on end. The corporation didn't seem to want to move the bus. 'Too dangerous', they said, 'to try moving burnt-out buses left up our way. Too many paramilitaries knocking about the place making themselves busy, making themselves important, finding wee jobs for themselves, poking their noses in, asking for money for this and that.'

'Any excuse,' my mother always said; 'they'd use any excuse to get out of a bit of work.'

So the bus lay there. Only the charred springs of the seats were left visible inside the bus. Everything else had turned into black dust and been blown out through the empty, melted windows. Or been stolen. One or the other. I didn't really know if there was anything worth stealing on a bus. I didn't get there quick enough to find out.

'Don't worry, there'll be another one along in a minute,' said the old man who lived opposite whenever you looked inside it to see if there was anything there worth taking. He must have sat there watching out for someone to approach it. I thought he was half-mad. I'd leave as soon as he started his little routine.

'Don't worry . . .' he'd shout.

'Fuck off, you mad cunt,' I'd shout back, quietly to myself.

'. . . there'll be another one along in a minute.'

'Fuck off, you mad auld cunt with nothing better to do with your time than shout shite at boys like me.'

I left school that June day and I legged it back to my street, where nobody worked and some waited all day by burnt-out buses to make their little crack before they disappeared inside again to wait for a few more hours until their next target turned up.

My mother thought this old neighbour of ours was quite funny. 'He's always got a ready quip at hand,' she'd say. 'He's quite witty really. They can't take our sense of humour away from us,' she always said. 'At least we can laugh at ourselves. Not like some people.' That was her little crack at the English, who were renowned for not being able to laugh at themselves. I couldn't see anything funny about it. He always said the same thing. She didn't have to listen to it all day. It was sad rather than funny, a very fucking sad way to see the day in. But that was just my view.

The really funny thing is that it came back to me when I got home. Stevenage. That was the name of the town built on a grid pattern. That's what I was searching for. Fucking Stevenage. I never went back to school after that. They wrote to me, but I never replied. The letters were addressed to my mother but I got there first. I had nothing to say – no excuse, no special plea, nothing. She was surprised that they never tried to get in contact with me. She said that she knew that they would soon enough.

So now I had a different routine. My job now was to put the potatoes on at ten to five. She'd peel them the night before, and leave them in a pot of water on the gas cooker ready for me. I'd light the gas at exactly ten to five and then get out of the house before she got back. Round the park, until she cooled down. As long as I wasn't in when she got home. She had never forgiven me for walking out like that. I'd passed the Eleven Plus so she had high expectations, the whole street had. For a while I was a local celebrity, Mrs Abbott gave me fifty pence for passing. I got into that school, and then I threw it all away. My mother was smart, she could have done all that I had done, but she didn't get the chance. Her parents wanted her out working, they wanted her in the mill. This was where all the anger came from. Now I had thrown in the towel, and there wasn't even a mill for me to go to. There was only work for women there, and work for men like Ernie. Men who could get on with everyone, men with good contacts.

I knew who made the call that finished it all. It was one of the lads who knocked about with me. He didn't mean any harm. He always told me that he was going to do it one day. It wasn't a threat, it was just a promise of a favour. He thought I'd appreciate the chance to beak off a lesson, he thought I would be thrilled with the opportunity to enjoy a free afternoon in the sun in early June. Even though it was raining that day. But I never brought it up with him. I couldn't face it.

The crows were circling overhead in the park. I could never work out what set them off. It would all be nice and quiet and then they'd be off squawking and screeching and getting excited about God knows what. Once they were out of their sharp, dark, tangled nests they made themselves busy. One of them would go into a litter bin, the rest would wait for him to come out. I watched one large bedraggled crow drag some greasy paper right out of a bin and across the grass. The rest were in a noisy line behind it, jostling and complaining and every so often catching up with the first bird, and snatching lumps of paper stained with fat away from it. *Cak, cak, cak*, then silence, as they wrestled and tugged the paper out of each other's beaks. Then more loud cries.

I prodded the damp earth with a long stick. The leaves were turning brown, with darker speckles in the middle, like dead butterflies caught on invisible flypaper on the ground, the dead wings stuck on some dried sludgy paste to the hardening earth. The dead wings of the leaves crackled as I prodded them with the stick. Some pencil-thin old man came towards me with a hard turd-shaped dog with short, bony, cantilevered legs. The crows parted for him to walk through, but they didn't fly off for him. They were far too busy.

The man's cheeks were hollow and unshaven, covered in a white downy hair. His shirt was done up to the top, but he had no tie. His jacket was the top half of a suit. It wasn't the same colour as his trousers. His trousers didn't fit. They were pulled in at the waist with an old light brown leather belt with matadors on it. The bull had his head down, the matador had his cape in one hand, a short sword in the other. It was the moment before the matador jabs the knife in. I had seen a bullfight on television once, you need to stab the bull a lot of times to put it down. You need to jab the sword in again and again and again into that thick gristly body. Human bodies have a lot of gristle too. I knew that from the lads I knocked about with. They told me all about it. Stabbing somebody isn't easy. It looks easy, but it isn't, they'd say. It might have been all talk, of course. I had never seen anybody getting stabbed, but then I had my homeworks to do. I wasn't with them all the time.

But people are very gristly, they're full of gristle. I was starting to notice that myself. Bulls must be even worse. The matador was so thin he was nearly a matchstick, but he managed to get his sword right into all that heaving perspiring gristle. The bull was fat and swollen and very angry. And bloody from all that stabbing.

A bull with a crimson body. A dozen crimson bulls around the belt of that old wizened man, pulling his dog along.

The old man's trousers looked as if they had been bought for a bigger man. An older brother perhaps, recently deceased, leaving a full wardrobe of clothes which he wouldn't have wanted to go to waste. Or perhaps, the trousers had been bought for that man himself, the man he had once been. It was impossible to tell.

But it was the jacket of his best suit, the suit for weddings and funerals, all its revels and public sadnesses done. It was the jacket for taking the dog out now. He was past the rest. All griefs would be private now. His family and friends were long gone. He would still have to mourn, but it would be on his own from now on, with his head buried in his chest, with the auld dog looking up at him, trying to understand, wondering what time its dinner would be ready.

He gave me that look. I was sure he recognized me but he didn't say hello. He just snorted, as if he couldn't be bothered wasting a greeting on the likes of me. The snort cleared his windpipes, and it acted as some sort of acknowledgement.

I could hear him coming before I saw him. Sucking in the breath, the air whistling as it left that bony, white chest. A lifetime up in the mill, before it became a thread factory. Sucking in the flax dust, trying to whistle as he worked. He had a lifetime in that dry dusty place, and he wanted me to be there on that bright dry afternoon, to understand what life is really all about. It was a pity that the mill was really just a big store room for thread now, and that Belfast linen had gone the way of Sheffield steel, and no doubt Paris buns, for all I cared: made somewhere else for half the price so that the likes of me could be left alone. They didn't really make anything up there any more, not in the way they once had done, not in the way they had made linen out of flax. Irish linen, the best in the world, was made up there from something that grew in our own native fields. But they didn't really make anything any longer. They just changed the thread around a bit, they put it on to reels and packed it and sent it off somewhere else. Nobody knew where exactly, that was the responsibility of the packing department, and the girls from the packing department were a bit odd, they didn't have a smoke and a wee chat with the rest of the girls at breaks. They kept themselves to themselves. They were very quiet. I thought they might be Roman Catholics from the way they behaved, but I was wrong, they were just quiet. Their personality was a bit different, that's all. It was nothing political.

I could feel his resentments, I could feel the old man looking straight at me. He pulled the dog along by its lead, its leaden chest rocked from side to side as it walked. The dog wasn't the height of two daisies, except when it shat,

37

which it did often, arching its thick gristly back for maximum relief. He tugged at it as it went into that position. The two of them straining. They stopped just by me. Even the dog glowered my way, as if I was responsible for its discomfort.

I watched the two of them walk off, pulling against each other. They had their routine, I had mine. I'd go off in a few minutes and sit on a swing, and wait until about six. She'd have been in then for about an hour, the dinner would be ready and she'd assume that I was out doing something, perhaps even looking for a job. She'd have calmed down. I would tell her that it's different these days. There's no work, I'd say, for seventeen-year-old lads in Belfast with no real qualifications, a few GCSEs hardly counted for anything. You just want to sit on your arse all day, is what she'd say. You've no interest in work. We'd have that fight. Like that man and his dog, pulling against each other.

I was sitting there on the swing, lying right back, my eyes closed, nearly dreaming, when somebody crept up right beside me. 'Bang, bang. You're fucking dead,' somebody shouted in my ear.

I jumped, my head hitting the rusty, metal chain of the swing. It was Billy Goodyear. Rubber Man we called him. His da was called Sammy Goodyear. His nickname was Rubber Man as well. A generation ago they made the same old jokes. Rubber Man had got married recently and he had his bride of three months and his baby with him. None of us had been invited to the wedding. The wife was a sad-eyed little thing in a short, tight pink skirt, and a blue top. She looked as if she cried a lot. You could see her belly sticking out through the thin material of the skirt, in a hard regular lump. It would take a few months for that to go down, I thought to myself. The bump looked more noticeable because the rest of her was so thin, except her tits which were swollen and heavy-looking. The baby slept soundly in its pram. Billy motioned towards it with one short sharp jabbing movement, as if to get the introductions over quickly.

'The baby,' he said.

'His name's Ben,' she added quietly.

She was annoyed that he hadn't mentioned his name. My gaze was drawn towards her eyes. Big grey eyes, the colour of the sea on a bad day. Not a cold greyness, just a sodden murky sort of greyness. Like Belfast Lough in late November. I'd seen that greyness. I'd mitched off primary school once and got the bus to Greencastle. I sat on the damp seaweed and shingle on the vacant shore. I'd planned to have a swim, until I noticed how the sea spewed up the ripped seaweed and the rubber tyres, gnawed by the waves and the salt. And how it dragged the bits of mangled wood on to the shingle, as if it was pulling these old broken unwanted things relentlessly out of the bottom of some bin, like some stray dog looking for food, and tossing them out in front of you. Like Mrs Shovelton when she threw old Sammy Shovelton's clothes out on the street, and told him to take himself off. His clothes lay there on the street for two days. Not a bit of wonder he didn't pick them up. They were shabby, even by the standards of our street. Every time the two of them had a fight, we'd go out on to the street to watch. All the fights were public up our way.

And then that day on the shore I noticed a Durex, milky from last night's pleasure and a day of being washed inside and out with salty water. I didn't even try to go into the water after that. I sat there staring at that greyness for a whole afternoon, listening to the rhythmic noise of the waves crashing on the shingly beach. I felt becalmed. It was a strange feeling. I left my schoolbag on the bus home. I didn't do this on purpose. It might have looked like this, but it wasn't done on purpose. It was an accident, a slip, a lapse of memory. I got the cane for that. It was only the second time that I'd ever got the cane. The first was for using a catapult. It wasn't my catapult but I owned up to having some of the pellets for it. I just had some of them in my pocket. I was looking after them for somebody, but I still got caned for that. The day after I got back from Greencastle, the headmaster took me into the room that they used when the nurse called to check for headlice. He made me close the door behind me. The cane was hidden away behind a chair, with the seat ripped, with the foam spewing out. The room had a poster of a boy with ginger hair smiling, showing his teeth, eating an apple. The headmaster gave me six strokes three on each hand. He flicked the hand out with the tip of the cane to make sure that it was fully extended. The tips of the fingers are very sensitive. After he had finished I thrust my fingers up into my armpits to get some relief. I could feel the sweat trickling down from my armpit. The heat there made my fingers throb more.

The headmaster told me, while he was doing it, that he only used the cane under extreme provocation since it was banned, and that he couldn't tolerate boys taking themselves off to Greencastle for the day. My mother would never have done that. He told me not to talk about it. I told my mother about me getting the cane, but she just said that I must have deserved it, whatever it was for. The headmaster was right to keep the cane handy for behaviour like mine, she said. After that I worked hard at school. Sometimes it felt like I was doing it just for spite, but sometimes I knew that I really wanted to get on, to make something of myself, to get well away from this sad, stupid place.

The baby was making some noise, not trying to cry, it was a more pleasant sound than that, as if it was just amusing itself making little noises. Billy looked uninterested. His wife was trying to smile, trying to haul the corners of the mouth up into something friendly and sincere. The muscles around her eyes never moved, as if she knew that there was no point in even trying. Billy was smiling widely, a great big open grin, his eyes crinkled and narrow. He had noticed some new graffiti on the grey slab of a wall.

'Ha! Ha! Ha! Darky. Rot in hell.' He read it out slowly.

'Who was Darky?' Grey eyes asked.

'Some fucking IRA bastard from the Falls,' said Billy. 'We got him all right. He walked right into it. That's what I heard. Right slap bang into it.'

'He wasn't just some random Catholic then?' she asked. 'Some poor innocent man going home to his family?'

She was looking at him almost accusingly. Then she looked at me. I noticed that her eyes had lost their sadness now. There was a steeliness about her, but only for a few seconds, a transient sort of steeliness. You could imagine that she could be awkward in a row. It was a different side to her, but short-lived. She looked less pathetic when she gave you that look, almost attractive.

'That's what the *Belfast Telegraph* said,' she said. 'I remember reading that in the paper at the time. It stuck in my mind. He had a young family. He was on his way home. He had two young sons. Women remember these kinds of things, you know. Women always remember details about young families. It's in our nature to be interested.'

'The papers always get it wrong,' said Billy; 'they're biased against us. And as for the TV, my ma says you have to be a Taig even to get an interview for a job there. Have you ever seen the names of the newsreaders on Ulster Television, or the names of the presenters? It's always Eamonn this and Roisin that. Every last one of them. What chance have poor wee Protestants got in this town?'

Billy pulled a large felt-tip out of his pocket. 'I keep this for emergency use only.'

RUBBER MAN. I'LL BE BACK.

'Bouncing right back,' said Billy. He was making his public statement in the only way that he knew how.

Billy and I started laughing. She said we were like a couple

41

of schoolboys. He looked happy, relieved to have bumped into one of his old mates. I heard he wasn't getting out much. Since he got married he had moved nearly a mile away, down to a house somewhere off the Stonepark, nobody knew exactly where. This was a little strange. For a number of reasons. Nobody moved away like that, we stayed in our neighbourhood. And that wasn't the only strange thing about him these days. His wife was called Sha.

'What kind of name is that?' my mother had asked me when she heard of the great event. 'Is it short for Sharon or is it Shah, as in the Shah of Persia?'

So I had asked him. 'It's short for Shannon,' he told me, which only made matters worse.

'Shannon as in River Shannon, the river that flows down south?' I asked.

'So what's wrong with that?' said Billy. Billy could anticipate what was coming next. He wasn't slow. 'King Billy was a Dutchman, but that doesn't make me Dutch because I've been named after him.'

I hadn't made up my mind about Sha, as she stood there looking miserable. I was never sure where Billy had actually met her. The details were very vague. He always said that it was in Kelly's, but we'd been barred from Kelly's for the past year. So I never believed anything that he told me about their first meeting. But there he was, grinning away, as if he hadn't a care in the world.

'I wanted to show Sha where we grew up. We used to get up to some right tricks here.'

Sha tried desperately to smile, as her eyes flitted across the graffiti about Darky and Malachy, the IRA bomber killed by his own bomb. REST IN PIECES it said. And Hawkeye, the UVF commander, serving life for his country. OUT OF SIGHT, BUT NOT OUT OF MIND. Someone had written TOO TRUE in big, black capitals at the bottom of this, and then someone else had added TRUE BLUE, with the T in red, the R in white

42

and the U in blue and so on right to the end, or nearly to the end. The last two letters were both in blood red with red drops underneath. I think that it was meant to look like dripping blood, to make the whole thing look a bit more sinister, but I couldn't be sure. The paint might just have run.

Billy pointed at the rocket and what remained of the wee Wendy hut at the top of the seven rusty steps. The seven steps to heaven we called them.

'You'll never guess what we used to do up there,' said Billy, to his sad-looking wife.

He was looking at me conspiratorially, lasciviously all out of the side of his face. He had a great knack of displaying two quite discrepant expressions at once. A lot of people when they met him for the first time thought that was why he was called Rubber Man. I could feel myself blushing. Shannon looked embarrassed. She looked down at the grey uneven concrete base to this child's playground. She looked quite pretty from that angle. But when she looked you straight in the face, it was hard to see the prettiness behind that awful bewildered expression.

The truth was that I had been in that hut with a girl just once, just the once. And there were three of us in there with her. We had tricked Marion Thompson up those steps, and as soon as we got her into the Wendy hut, Hammerhead had skunked up those rusty steps behind her, nudged her into our little den and grabbed her through her sweater. When I say we tricked her in, it was really left up to me. She wouldn't have gone anywhere near the Wendy hut if she'd known that Hammerhead and Billy were about. She trusted me. 'You're very plausible,' my mother would always tell me. It was both a compliment and an accusation. I think Marion may have even fancied me.

I asked her to go up there with me then Hammerhead and Billy ran up after us, and bundled the pair of us into

43

the dark bit at the back of this dank little hut with its damp stained wet wood. She screamed, when she realized what was happening, and kept screaming as Billy and Hammerhead pushed in between me and her.

I couldn't join in, I knew her brother too well. I used to sit beside him in primary school. He had grown up with three younger sisters, and so he had always been considered something of an expert on the female body. One day he said to me 'Do you know what a girl's fanny looks like?' I shook my head. He rolled up his sleeve and crooked his arm, and said, 'Just like that – a wee slit, a wee bare slit.'

I felt that I knew Marion already. I could never look at her without thinking about that wee bare slit. She was screaming as Hammerhead tried to get her top off. I just caught sight of her bra and her big, milky white tits. I said that I had to go for a pish, and I could hear her screams echoing around the Wendy hut. I didn't really need a pish, and when I pulled it out it was hard, so I just stood there with it in my hand listening to her sobbing, waiting for it to go down. I wanted to put my fingers in my ears. I didn't want to listen to the girl with the wee bare slit. Then it went quiet. By the time I got back it was all over. Whatever it was.

I say whatever it was because I hadn't had sex yet. The lads didn't know that. I'd hear them up the entry with their girls when I was doing my homeworks. I'd wank in time to the noises from behind the entry wall. I thought it was like having sex, which in a way it was. I knew the tempo of sex, the rhythm, the timing. It was very quick. At least I had learnt something. It was just the feelings I didn't know anything about, the emotions, the senses, the sensations, except the release at the end, that sudden sharp feeling that doesn't satisfy, that just makes you want to start all over again. One night, I wanked off eleven times until it started bleeding. Not because I'd heard anybody doing it eleven times. I just started in time with a couple I couldn't see, and then I found that I couldn't really stop. It was a break from the Latin. I left it alone for a few days after that. Not the Latin, the other thing.

Marion had calmed down, she scrambled down the rusty steps past me, as I made my way up. She wouldn't look me in the eye. But I could see that she was still sobbing, and trying to draw a breath through the thick sobs. Billy was lying back in the corner, trying to light a cigarette with a half a match. A match that had splintered all the way up. But it was all he had left.

'Where the fucking hell have you been?' he said, as I came in crouching low to get through the door. 'She settled down after a few seconds. You should have stayed.'

Hammerhead snatched the bit of match off him and struck it on the sole of his shoe. It lit first time. He cupped his hand around it and lit Billy's cigarette.

'Hammerhead may have got the tit first, but he just ended up with sloppy seconds. Isn't that right?' said Billy.

Hammerhead just gave a big dirty grin.

'And you got fuck all,' said Billy. 'Did you have to go for a pish? I can't do it if I'm busting to go. It's funny that.'

They were sitting side by side in the Wendy hut, their legs extended in front of them, facing the side, looking out through the slits in the wood. I crouched in the doorway watching them, and then pushed in beside them. The hut smelt of old damp wood and new sweat. It was very quiet in there, you could hear some dog barking aimlessly in the distance, otherwise all I could hear was Hammerhead's deep breathing. He was out of breath.

Hammerhead pulled up his shirt and wrote BORN TO FUCK with a green felt-tip pen across the lower part of his abdomen. You could see his bushy ginger pubes peeking out of his pants.

'I'm thinking of having this tattooed here,' he said. 'I'm

a natural lover.' He grabbed hold of my shirt and held me with his left hand and tried to get the buttons open with his right. 'I'm going to write "Born to get fuck all" on your fucking belly,' he said. 'If I don't see you doing it soon, I'm going to assume that you're a puff.'

I wrestled free and moved away slightly so that we were no longer touching. Suddenly, he burst out laughing.

'Only kidding. We got fuck all today. Billy was chatting away to her, trying to calm her down, stroking her hair. She was terrified. Him stroking her hair only made her worse. He was whispering all these things in her ear – "You're so beautiful. You're really gorgeous. You've got the biggest fucking tits I've ever seen." This was meant to calm her down. He was trying to get his fingers up her flue at the same time.'

Billy flicked the butt of the cigarette through the wooden panels of the Wendy hut. He was looking into the distance, as if he was thinking about other more important things, as if he was ignoring the insults about his ability to talk to girls.

'Hammerhead would have been useless anyway,' he said, still looking out. 'There were all these drops of water at the end of his wee skinny dick. He would have shot his watery load before he even got into her.' He had turned to face us now. 'He wouldn't have shot his load, he'd have had to drip it.'

'He'd have had to spray it,' I said, not wanting to be left out of the crack. 'That's what you do with water isn't it? You spray it.'

'Yes, but he didn't have a hose,' said Billy. 'Just a wee thimbleful of watery paste. I know: we'll call him Thimble Dick in future.'

'And we'll call you the chimney sweep,' said Hammerhead. 'The only man I know who makes a mess every time he tries to get up a flue.'

They were both laughing away, whilst Marion no doubt

slipped sobbing into her house and up the stairs before anyone noticed her torn blouse and soiled skirt.

And there standing in the park that afternoon I could see Billy's eyes dart this way and that, reliving the good old days in the Wendy hut, before he settled down, with some little girl who cried a lot and his baby in a house somewhere off the Stonepark Road. In some anonymous street, which he liked to keep secret, so that his friends couldn't visit. I told him it was time for my dinner and I left him and his sad-eyed wife listening to the noises that crows make when they're very excited, but they've nowhere to go.

3

When I got home, she had already started her dinner. Mine was in the oven. She didn't look up. She was watching the news. 'It's ruined,' she said. 'Put it in the bin. That's all it's bloody good for. Put it in the bloody bin. Do you want me to go over and do it for you?' She stood up as if she was going to go into the kitchen and get it, but she was only bluffing. She sat back down again, her eyes all the time on the television. Not once did she look at me.

I went and got it out of the oven. It smelt burnt. The beans, sausages and potatoes had a thin, light crust over the top. I carried the plate in with a tea-towel saying *Culdaff – great food, great people, great times* on it. I sat on the pouffe in front of the television, and spread the tea-towel over my knee. I could feel the plate burning through the thin tea-towel. I cut through the light oven-baked crust, and some steam came out, making a gentle whooshing noise like a diver finding air. The dinner was ruined. She was right about some things. I started eating slowly from the edge of the plate, working my way around the circumference. She didn't look at me, as I started nibbling at the crust on the potatoes. There was silence for a moment. Then it started.

'Where the hell have you been?'

The question rushed out of her mouth, as if the whole thing had been assembled in some store and was just waiting there in an anteroom to be pushed out head-first and fully formed. Clipped stabbing syllables. This was no question.

No genuine question was ever put together like this. I wanted to ask her where she thought I might have been. There were so many alternatives. I told her that I had been talking to Billy Goodyear.

'I knew his da. He was no good either. The whole family are like that. No bloody good.'

I told her that he had had a baby.

'What's his wife's name again?'

I said that I couldn't remember. I didn't want another argument. The television flickered in the corner.

The local news had an item about a punishment beating in North Belfast. Some lad was dragged from his home and beaten with sticks with nails in them. I didn't recognize his name. But the house looked familiar enough. It was like ours, small, compact, done up by the Housing Executive. The toilet taken out of the yard, and put into the house. His attackers came in through the yard, they kicked down the back door. It lay off its hinges. The door had splintered, like an orange crate. Cheap, thin wood. Housing Executive wood.

My mother sat squinting at the screen. 'I see they made a right mess in there,' she said. 'Look at that kitchen. I bet it was lovely before they came in. Look at that bloody mess on the floor.'

She sat watching the TV, offering up her commentary. It was mostly about the house, and the broken crockery and the stains on the carpet. The TV flickered, as if it might turn itself off, but then it burst back to life. She'd bought the TV for forty pounds and it had never worked properly, but you couldn't say that. You had to squeeze the muscles around your eyes to try to get the picture into focus. Wee Joe Robinson used to fix her previous black-and-white machine, and he had recommended a friend who did up old obsolete colour TV sets, and sold them cheap. Real bargains, except they never worked. She had told me that wee Joe was on the disability now, that he was nearly blind. But he still popped in now and again to have a fiddle with our television.

We sat in front of the television, our dinners on our laps, squinting at the TV in the corner, the TV recommended by a blind repairman.

'You'd wonder what that lad would have done to deserve that,' she said, pointing at the prostrate image on the screen. She left a gap, inviting me in. She was looking for a row. Punishment beatings were always a good bet. There was always plenty to disagree about. 'But he must have done something.

'The Organization don't do those sorts of things to you for nothing. He'd have got plenty of warnings. That's how they work, you know. They give you plenty of warnings. Plenty of opportunities to change your ways.'

The news footage lingered on still photographs of his injuries, sharp little puncture holes in his arms and legs, each little hole surrounded by reddened purple skin. Two in his neck, a dozen in the back of his hands where he tried to protect his face. The hands were heavy with swelling, black and purple.

'Those two on his neck look like insect bites,' said my mother out of the blue. 'Like wee midge bites.'

He was about my age. When he spoke he had a surprisingly high voice. It made his accent even more pronounced, every statement he made sounded like some incredulous question. He said that it was a case of mistaken identity. But given his accent and his high voice, it came out like no assertion at all, just a long rising question to his assailants out there, sitting perhaps in a room like this one, with their dinners on their knee.

She sat there laughing, but it wasn't a real laugh. It was a laugh as commentary, it was a laugh as accusation.

'Who does he think he's talking to?' she said. 'Does he really believe that we'll fall for that old line? The Organization don't make those kinds of mistakes. They have intelligence on all these characters. They do their homework, and the cowboys on the street know that. You can't get away with any nonsense with the Organization, you know.'

I knew all about the men in the Organization. Kingo's da was in, and Jimmy's brother. I would watch them going into the bookie's with the rest of the mugs. They had more readies to throw around, but they lost it like the rest of them. Jimmy's brother was all right though. When I was a kid, we had been messing about the quarries and the siren had gone off. Everybody ran off, and left me behind. I was the youngest. Jimmy's brother came back for me, and carried me on his back. His neck had smelt of talcum powder. I don't know if I'd have been killed by the blast if he hadn't come back for me, but I would have been covered in limestone dust and probably killed later by my mother. Jimmy's brother was always a bit of a hero to me after that, but he had his failings. The talcum powder for a start.

I also knew for a fact that he couldn't swim. I had seen him round at the dam at the back of the mill one late afternoon, making all these excuses as to why he couldn't go into this lonely weedy pond where a man had drowned. Then somebody gave him a nudge and he had gone down into the oily water. He hauled himself on to the pipe in the middle of the dam and refused to get back into the water, until his pal Freddy Fog, as we called him, went to fetch him. He came back on Freddy's shoulders, laughing and shouting and acting the big man, as if it was all a joke, but we all knew that he wouldn't come back on his own.

I knew other things about the Organization. The rumours, the stories we told each other, the messages they left for us on our gable wall. We sometimes watched the words go up, as the messages were painted on in bright bold letters.

51

THE UVF RESERVE THE RIGHT
TO STRIKE AT REPUBLICAN TARGETS
WHERE AND WHEN
THE OPPORTUNITY ARISES

That was an old faded one in red, white and blue. The blue
was like washed-out denim, white in patches. I remember
this being done when I was a boy one sunny afternoon in a
warm June. This stranger turned up in some overalls to do
it, as if it was a proper job, but he ran out of paint and had
to go and fetch some more.

Mrs Henderson came along and told him off for vandaliz-
ing our gable wall. She was angry because he was some out-
sider brought in to keep us in line. That's how she described
it. My mother made him a cup of tea. She said that he was
only doing his job. He had three sugars in his tea. I remember having to get him that third sugar.

We were all standing there in the street watching him,
trying to guess what right the UVF were reserving. He ran
out of paint after the first line, but he wouldn't tell us what
was coming next. He had a wee note in front of him, which
he was copying. But he kept that well covered. It took him
ages to finish the whole thing. He was trying to make the
lettering look more interesting, with little curls at the end
of each letter.

Wee Sammy Spade – that's what we called him; I didn't
know Samuel's real name, he lived two streets away – asked
the painter if we would be allowed to kick our football against
the wall, now that it had been painted. The painter told him
that it would be all right, as long as the ball didn't hit the
mural and knock chips off it. If it did then we'd be in trouble.
Wee Sammy always kicked his football against the gable wall
in the next street after that.

It still wasn't his own gable wall, mind. My mother said
that he never used his own gable wall. His mother didn't

allow him. He always used somebody else's. My mother was pleased that the mural on our wall stopped him from using ours.

The painter told us that it was his first official wall mural, but it wasn't really a mural at all. Just a threat.

And that night, sure enough, a coincidence no doubt, some Catholic lad walking home with his girlfriend was picked up just off the Crumlin and shot in the head and dumped on the side of the road up above the glen. His girlfriend was allowed to go home on her own. There were pictures of her in the paper squealing her head off. I never saw the body, but there was a brown stain which stayed in the cracks in the pavement for weeks. We all went on our bicycles to see the mark and to feel the texture of the pavement where his body was dumped.

'Imagine your head hitting that,' Colin would say, rubbing the rough concrete. 'Imagine the thump.'

We would spend hours arguing whether it would be a thump or a crack. We would tap our own heads on the concrete to hear the sounds.

'But the car would be moving when your man was thrown out,' Colin would remind us; 'that would make a difference.' So we would try throwing ourselves off our bicycles to see if that would make the sound different.

After the mark had gone Bobby Wylie used to pour Ribena into the cracks so that we would have something to go and look at on cold wet nights. He denied this, of course, but every now and then the stigmata would reappear stronger than before. The only problem was that it was more purple than brown. Bobby was always very keen on the spot because it wasn't very far from his house. He liked living somewhere dangerous.

One night I found some hairs in a crack in the pavement just by the Ribena mark. I think they may have belonged to the lad who was dumped there. I kept them in my pencil case, and showed them to the boys at school. Nobody ever believed me. Bobby may have put them there as well. You couldn't be sure about these things. Colin said that there should be some skin attached to them if they were the genuine article.

The particular stretch of gable wall bearing the threat had never been repainted, which I always thought was just as well. I didn't really want any more coincidences.

Then there were the proper murals telling us about the Organization. 'Real art,' my mother said, but she always called them 'murials'.

UFF
ROCKET TEAM
ON TOUR
WEST BELFAST

That was down on Snugville Street. There was a very fancy gold and red crown above the Red Hand of Ulster. Then a Latin inscription: QUIS SEPARABIT. I was the only one at the corner who could translate that. They would get me to do my Latin for them. They'd say, 'Do your Latin for us,' and I'd go, '*Dominus, domine, dominum, domini, domino, domino. Mensa, mensa, mensam, mensae, mensae, mensa.*' It was my party piece. Billy could pish right over the top of the toilet wall at primary school, and I could decline Latin nouns. Girls would come in to watch him. The boys at the corner would tell me that I had a powerful memory, but they would tell Billy that he had a powerful pump. I knew which they would have preferred for themselves.

Kingo went one better, by telling us all that the UFF guy with the rocket launcher in the mural was modelled on his da. But it couldn't have been because the guy on the mural didn't have a beer gut. But he did have the right sort of hard eyes peeking through his balaclava. Kingo said that the mural was done from a photograph of his da when he was younger. The guy with the rocket launcher was wearing a grey hooded top under his black jacket. I always thought he looked quite trendy. Not like Kingo's da at all.

Then there were the hastily painted notes aimed at kids like us. THIEVES WATCH OUT. DRUG DEALERS BEWARE. THERE IS NO HIDING PLACE FOR DELINQUENTS IN OUR COMMUNITY. I never saw any of these being painted, but there was a rumour that some of the shopkeepers used to come out at night to do these, just to keep us in our place. But whenever we read about punishment beatings delivered to anti-social elements in the community, we knew deep inside that this was just a rumour.

And then there were the reminders that the Organization were not all talk, that there was more to all this than a bit of community art or the outpourings of a bored graffiti artist. Gino, the IRA man, was hit down in the social security office. Some smart guy wrote GINO SIGNED OFF AT LAST.

It always made sense to read what was on the walls. We put up our own markers. TARTAN GANGS RULE, YOUNG DEFENDERS, HAMMERHEAD IS A WANKER, THE BIG E. But nobody ever seemed to notice our little signs. They never mentioned them. But they must have seen them because every now and again somebody would come along during the night and throw paint over them, blotting out who we were. What we stood for.

She was still going on about the Organization. She would always go on about the men from the corner all out during the Loyalist Workers Strike, standing in their uniforms behind roadblocks. She was impressed by the military precision of the whole thing. The marching, the drill with baseball bats, the barking-out of orders. But more than that she was impressed by the fact that some of the officers had English accents. The UDA were professionals, run by men with English accents. Men who knew what they were doing.

My friend, Chuckie, knew who this one character with the English accent really was. The Englishman, who looked so professional in his balaclava. It was Norman Finlay. He was born in Birmingham all right, but he came to Belfast looking for work because he couldn't get a job in Birmingham. His parents were from Belfast. I tried to explain all this to her once, but she never let me finish. 'What do you know, you little shite, you can't even get a job.'

She was still drawn to the TV. 'And this frigging wee yahoo wants us to believe that they run around pulling innocent boys out of their houses and knocking the shite out of them. Who does he think he's talking to?' She lifted my plate, and went into the kitchen. 'That's right, you just sit there. Don't bother moving.'

I could hear her dumping the plates in the sink. 'There's no pleasure in eating here any more. You just come in when you want to, rush it down you and then you're out.

'It's not like when your father was alive.'

She had been building up to this. Her voice was starting to crack with emotion. I could feel the same emotional surge within me, trying to bubble up and sweep across me. I forced myself to dampen it down.

My father died on a wet Sunday on the Falls Road. In a hospital sure enough, but it was still the Falls. Just another reason to hate that stretch of Belfast, that Fenian hole. I was told half-way across the car park with my Aunty Diane on the way to see my mother. Wet puddles, a misty night. She was on my left. I always remember that. You can always remember the positions of things. It's funny, that. My uncle came out of the hospital between two cars, a red Ford beside a blue car. I can't remember what make the blue car was. Me with such a powerful memory as well. I've tried thinking about it and I've even tried drawing it, but it's no good. I've even tried dreaming about it. I've thought about it deliberately before going to sleep so the dreams would take over and take me back there. But I can't get the shape of that blue car into my mind.

I stepped in a puddle. I do remember that. My feet were wet. I can feel them wet now, wet right through. I was just shaking my shoe when I saw my uncle. I knew that it was bad news from the expression on his face. His expression was locked on his face, like he had to try very hard to control it. He wouldn't look at me. He started crying as soon as he started to talk. It was as if the words set him off. He was all right as long as he wasn't talking.

I had never seen him crying before. Or since. He didn't cry at my da's funeral. But he was ready for that, he was geared up for it. He just put on his suit and black tie and did everything slowly and carefully, with great precision. He didn't cry. Not a drop. Not one fucking drop. He might have had a drink to help him get through this.

I don't remember what he said that night in the car park. I just remember that he wouldn't look at me, and his cheeks were wet with tears. Of course, it could have been the rain. I've thought about that many times. Perhaps his cheeks were wet with the rain. But I've studied this closely, and I've concluded that the rain wouldn't cling to you like that. It wouldn't streak your cheeks the way salty tears would. And his cheeks were definitely streaked that night. I would stake my life on that. There were streaks down his cheeks. There were definitely big salty streaks from his eyes to his chin.

My father died of a bad heart. That's all anyone ever told me. He had a bad heart. What was bad about it, I don't know. He had to go into hospital for tests. For what I don't know. All I do know is that he was hoping to go into hospital and out again without telling us. Perhaps he thought that we might not notice. But he didn't want to worry us. That was the kind of man he was. The last words I said to him, as he lay in that hospital bed before his tests, were that our cat Tiddles had been run over by a milkfloat. It wasn't true, of course, it was just that I wanted to cheer him up by saying something shocking and then telling him it wasn't true after all. This is a little routine of mine, designed to make the world a more cheerful place. Say the worst, and then back-track. When my mother went off to talk to the nurse, I told him that I had found Tiddles squashed on our street, and that I only recognized her from her collar.

He sat there in his pyjamas, his glasses in his pyjama pocket, and what little colour he had drained from his face. I felt bad when I had to tell him that it wasn't true. Here was a man with a bad heart. That was the last time I saw him alive. He came home a week later to lie in an open coffin below the lamp with the big pink shade and the cream tassels in the front room. I went into the kitchen until they got him into place. He didn't look very dignified until they got him settled. I never got a chance to see him in the hospital lying in a coma. I was too young. I wasn't too young to see him dead though. But that's different, they say.

'He's the best-looking corpse I've ever seen,' our next-door neighbour Lizzie said, when they brought him home. She was just trying to cheer us up. My mother always said that he looked so good because he died in good health. 'He just had an operation, and didn't come out of it.' I was sure that it was more to do with the pink lampshade and the pinkish glow on his waxen skin, but as usual I kept my mouth shut. Mary from two streets away, who was always drunk, tried to kiss him on the lips, just before they screwed the coffin lid down. My mother went hysterical.

That was my last image of him, as he left our house for ever. Mary being held by the fireplace by my uncle and her brother. She was trying to struggle out of her coat, streaked with old stains from drink and vomit, trying to get near my father just lying there. My mother, held by some anonymous hands, screaming his name over and over again. Two of my mates were waiting on the street to walk with me to Roselawn.

It was Tucker and Hammerhead, my best mates. I was glad they were there. They didn't say anything, they didn't need to. They just trooped in behind me to walk in the funeral cortège behind my father leaving our street for ever. You can depend on your mates. Tucker always told me afterwards that I wouldn't look at anybody on the day of the funeral, that I just kept my head down. He wasn't even sure that I knew he was there. But I knew all right. I don't think I could have walked without them, without making a fool of myself that is, without crying like a fucking baby, which I wasn't. I was twelve, not the sort of age where you can just cry in front of people. Like a wee fucking child.

That was five years ago. Before my father got a chance to teach me all the things that one day I might need to know. He had promised to teach me to dive. He said that one day he was going to teach me to dive into a pool and swim a width under water and then go right between his legs. But we never got round to it. When I went to the swimming baths on a Saturday morning with the lads from the corner I always jumped in. My pals always asked me why I didn't dive. I said I liked making a big splash. I said that I liked soaking people. Every time I went to the baths I thought about him.

My father died before he got a chance to go to church with us on a Sunday morning. I used to lie in bed and think about this. That had been important once. We weren't a good living family, but my mother took me to church and all three of us believed in hell. He always had a lie-in, and we would come home in our Sunday clothes smelling of mothballs, and I'd jump up and down on the bed next to him, and make his glasses fall off as he read the paper.

But he liked to hear me recite what I'd learnt in Sunday school. He'd sit up with the *News of the World* across his chest and his glasses on top of the paper, and I'd sit against the wooden board at the far end of the bed, and recite from memory.

> 'He makes me lie down in green pastures,
> he leads me beside quiet waters,
> he restores my soul.'

He was always proud of the way I talked from memory.

> 'I will fear no evil
> for you are with me.'

'That school will learn you to talk right. You'll come out sounding English,' he would say. He made me a little bronze medal with the name of the school on it the week before he went into hospital. He didn't get the name of the school right. He put the 'Royal' first. He called it the 'Royal Belfast School'. I wished he had asked me the name of the school before he had started doing the medal for me. He also made me a fake sovereign, and he wrote on one side 1 SOVEREION, and 1831 on the other. I don't think it would have fooled anybody. I had been hoping to use it one day.

My mother told me that as long as he had asked the Lord for forgiveness just before his operation he would be all right. He would be in heaven now waiting for us.

But I was worried because he didn't think that the tests were that dangerous beforehand. What happened if he thought that he would pray for forgiveness afterwards? What happened if he went to hell? Would I get a chance to see him there? Can you find your da in hell? How dark is it really down there? What would happen if I wasn't destined for hell, and he was down there waiting for me?

Up in our church, we didn't dwell on hell. We sat on the pew the second from the back below St Patrick in stained glass on the window, with yellow and green snakes around his sandals. Mrs Henderson would give us a polite smile. There were little red velvet cushions to kneel on for prayer, but boys like me never knelt. We just leant forward, our heads in our hands. We'd have a good look around us when we were praying. The church was full of women and children. The men were in bed, except for the old ones. But I had been to the mission hall on the corner. They knew all about hell. On a Monday night you got two lollies for going there. There wasn't much else to do, and it was warm so we went down to the wee mission hall occasionally. There was always a cartoon book on the seat just waiting for you. I remember one in which there was a Christian talking to another character, a patient in hospital dying of cancer. You could tell one was a Christian because of his blond good looks. The good-looking Christian tells the other fella about hell. He dwells on it. 'You won't be able to see your friends down there. It's a place of thick darkness. Sulphur has a dark flame. You'll have all your desires but they will never be satisfied. It will be horrible. You'll see no one.' The cancer victim, who always looked a little bit Mexican to me, tells him to go to hell. The Christian replies, 'I can't.' I always thought that the Christian was very smug about the whole thing.

The lads on the corner used to get me to recite this little story to them. We were ten years old at the time. It used to frighten the hell out of them. But I never forgot the story. So if my da went to the place of thick darkness, and I became a Christian, he might be down there trying to find me for eternity.

His voice had already faded in my memory. I saw a TV programme one night in which a hypnotist, or a hypnotherapist I think it was, said that human memory is a bit like a video recording of life, with all events stored, waiting to be played over and over again, if you just knew the right way in. If you just had the key to unlock them. But I knew that wasn't true, because no matter how hard I tried I just ended up with fragments – positions, colours and irrelevant details like streaked tears down the side of a face in the wind and the rain, or a blue car with a dent going rusty, the metal being eaten by rust like the worms in the ground gnawing away. Just fragments with no logic binding them together. No logic that I could see.

That afternoon up the Hightown with me kicking the ball about, him lying there reading the *Daily Mirror*, his glasses over the end of his nose. Me booting the ball up in the air and chasing it over the ground covered in prickly yellow gorse and loose, sharp brick. My thin-soled trainers – cheap ones bought down the Shankill for £5.99. And then me stumbling on a sliver of broken glass which somehow managed to pierce the side of my ankle. The little red hole, like that lad's who had had the punishment beating, like an insect bite. My father had to carry me back to the car. I remember him struggling with my weight. I don't remember how his voice sounded or what we talked about that day. I don't remember any of the meaningful stuff.

I can remember the make of the ball, and the fact that it was a Thursday, and who we saw on the way there, but I can't remember what he said, or how he spoke. I just remember him struggling under my weight, and wheezing with the effort. Just fragments really, ephemera. I also remember that his glasses dropped off on the way back, and that he had to put me down on the wet grass, while he picked them up. His glasses fell off a lot, the frames were loose.

I remember smells from him. That's the funny thing. Not any important messages from him or his voice, just smells. Engine oil, engine oil that's been on the road and seeped into old overalls. He worked with bus engines and smelt of the oil that they put into buses, even on his day off. Old overalls, weeks between washes. That's all I remember. I still like to pick up oily rags and hold them right up to my nose and to breathe deeply, to breathe him back to life. I was caught doing this once by an old woman round the back of a garage, she thought that I was a glue sniffer. She swore at me, and said she was going to ring the police.

The ankle went purple and septic two days after that Thursday up the Hightown. I remember the noise of the doctor's surgery, and the injection. I even remember how the doctor said 'take', which came out sounding like 'tack'. The doctor wasn't from our part of Belfast, in fact he wasn't from Belfast at all which is probably why I remember his funny accent. I can't remember my da's voice, but I can remember the doctor's odd pronunciation. It's funny that. Memory seems to be an arbitrary and cruel thing sometimes.

After his death, I wanted to keep his clothes as a way back to him. But my ma gave them all away to his brother. The brother had been drinking the day he came to collect them and he wouldn't come into the house. He smelt of drink the day of the funeral, and stayed out on the street then as well. It was a sweet, sickly smell, not like Black Bush or porter. I heard my mother say that he drank bottles of sherry. I never saw him in any of the clothes. Perhaps he couldn't bear to wear them; perhaps he didn't like them.

I wanted to keep just something of my father's. I scoured the cupboard above the TV, and the drawers in the front bedroom. I found the case of his glasses in the cupboard one afternoon in the bottom of a little wicker basket where my mother kept her sewing. The glasses had disappeared. So I kept the case. It didn't smell of him, it just smelt of old plastic, and the spring had gone so the case didn't snap shut the way it should have done. But I hid it in a shoebox under my bed, along with the plastic skittle which I'd filled with wet sand to make a cosh when I was still a boy, and some phials of drugs Billy and Hammerhead had stolen from the doctor's. They'd broken in one night, while I acted as look-out. But they didn't recognize what they managed to get, so

I hid some of the stuff for them until we could work out what it was. I'd been to the library to look up drugs, but they weren't in the book. But I thought I'd hang on to the drugs just in case they turned out to be something interesting. I kept all these forbidden things in the dark, dusty corner beneath my bed. I didn't want anybody to take them away from me. Nobody ever went under there.

The last shot of the lad on the television was of him being half carried along the corridor of the hospital by some nurse with dark hair and a big, fat arse. His ma trailed behind the two of them, looking angry.

My mother was sitting on the settee squinting at the TV still, slurping her tea, lowering her head for every drink. The teacup had a crack in it, and the tea had stained the crack brown. I told her that she should throw the teacup out, but she told me to mind my own business.

I said that I was going down to the corner for an hour. She didn't look up.

4

There were three lads there when I got down. I nodded and slipped automatically into my position beside them. I didn't say anything. Our backs up against the wall of the chip shop. We called it the corner, but it was really just the front of a chippie. The air vent blew out hot, pungent smells. I used to find these smells very nauseating. But I had grown used to them.

The four of us stood in a silent row, watching the traffic – the black taxis and the buses and the odd RUC or army patrol. Jackie gave the fingers to a passing RUC Land-Rover. The Land-Rover stopped but nothing happened. Then it accelerated away. An RUC man sitting in the back gave the same gesture back. I had been ready to run, in case they stopped. I had already rehearsed my route – down the side of the baker's, across the backs, careful about the broken glass on the left-hand side, down the entry beside the pigeon club, over the wall at the house on the end. Crouch in the corner of the yard of that house. The old woman who lived there never went into her yard. Wait for twenty minutes. Go home, carefully. I always liked to rehearse my escapes. That's why I had never been caught. I liked to plan things.

Jackie was beaming away.

'What did you do that for?' I asked.

'I felt like it,' said Jackie.

He stepped forward and took a little bow, as if he had just

done something worthy of critical acclaim, as if he had just done something. I noticed that he had got a new pair of Wrangler jeans on, and a new Levi jacket. He knew we would all notice them. That's why he was so full of himself.

'I've been shopping again,' he said. 'We went on a thieving spree on Saturday. It was dead easy.' He stepped forward again and ran his hand up and down the side of his new jeans.

'I just put these new jeans on in the shop and left my old ones on the hanger,' he said. 'My old ones had dog shite down the leg as well. It was a piece of cake. The Levi jacket just fell into my bag. The man in the shop saw me slipping it into my bag. I froze for a second, and then I just told him to shush. As if I was talking to a wee child. That's how you have to talk to some people – as if they're a wee one or a dog. It's very comforting for them. Then I showed him my hammer peeking out of my jacket. He just stared at it. You could see in his eyes that he was imagining what the hammer would feel like on his skull. That big heavy end making a big fucking dent on his head.'

And Jackie burst out laughing. And then we all did. Jackie slowly walked up and down in front of us modelling his new clothes. It was as if money was no object, which it wasn't to Jackie who was skilled in crowded shops.

'If I'd been pulled in by the RUC and they'd found the hammer, I'd just have told them I was coming from work,' said Jackie. He opened his eyes wide and raised the pitch of his speech. 'Honestly, mister, I'm on my way from work.'

'But you've never worked,' said Chuckie. 'You don't know what work is.' Chuckie was sounding like my mother.

'Yes, but they wouldn't know that,' said Jackie. 'They'd just have thought that here was a wee lad signing on the brew with a wee job on the side, a wee lad doing the double and trying to make something of himself. A wee lad who was so busy he had to go shopping in his work clothes covered in dog shite.'

He had us all smiling now. The cheek of it. You could go a long way with a bit of cheek, that's what my mother always said.

We saw wee Julie McGimpsey and her mother coming along. Julie was a year younger than me, her mother was in her early thirties. Both had tousled, blond hair, and short skirts. Their walk was almost identical. I had never noticed that before. Their strides were very short. Julie was a very early developer. She had breasts at primary school. Boys were always writing dirty notes to her. The headmaster found a note that Hammerhead had written to her. He got the cane for that in the headlice room with the door closed. We watched them come towards us, wobbling our way.

'Two fucking prick teasers,' said Chuckie out of the side of his mouth. 'Which would you have first?'

Four pairs of eyes burnt into their thin, viscose tops. I could make out the pattern on Julie's mother's bra first, I could see every flower, leaf and stalk on that black brassière, through that almost transparent top. Chuckie had both hands in the pockets of his jeans, squeezing himself hard. Julie said hello to me as she passed. And at that precise moment Chuckie took a sharp and very audible intake of breath through gritted teeth. So sharp and so loud that Julie's mother jumped.

'I'd have the mother first,' he said, as they passed. 'Definitely, the mother. Then Julie fucking cock teaser McGimpsey.'

We watched them go into the video shop, and I closed my eyes and tried to imagine a night in front of the TV with Julie and her mother.

'Did you know that Stokie wanked off old Jimmy Gordon's dog outside the bookie's last Friday?' asked Jackie.

His interjection broke the mood. Chuckie and Tom burst out laughing.

'He just did it for a laugh. He found this rubber glove, you see, so he thought he might as well use it for something. The glove was covered in oil, but that didn't matter. The dog didn't mind. The dog's tongue was hanging down to its balls after it was all over.'

We were still laughing when Kingo's da came past. He was a man in his early forties, tall with very dark hair that used to be swept back, but now it fell sideways across his head. Kingo had bought him some power gel for Christmas, but no matter how hard he tried the hair wouldn't go back the way it once had done, even with great dollops of gel for total control. He was tall and slim-hipped with broad shoulders like somebody from a western, but with this enormous beer gut. He was wearing jeans and the top half of a suit, with a blue Ben Sherman shirt underneath. He was still a good-looking man, but I had never seen him with Kingo's mother, who apparently never went out, except to her job in the dry cleaner's. Kingo's da was always out.

He was in the Organization, the UDA. We knew that because Kingo told us, and we had all seen something that could have been a uniform hanging up in his wardrobe one afternoon. Kingo had been bragging about his da being an officer in the Organization so often that one day we all said we wanted to see the proof. So we all trooped round to his house, and slipped through the front door one at a time, into the living room all pink and red and velvet and porcelain and gold plate. All crammed full and glinting. I had never been in his house before. I'd hung about outside the front door with the letterbox with the grille round it. 'Bomb-proof,' said Kingo, but I wasn't so sure. That was our space, the space just outside the door sheltering from the sideways rain, damp smells of wet clothing with the grown-ups edging past and muttering about how we never moved.

But this was my first time in that house, with its thick staircarpet smelling of carpet shops. And sure enough in the front room upstairs there was a green camouflage jacket and a little cap sitting neatly on a hanger, which could have been part of a uniform. There was a red, white and blue scarf as well, which Kingo said he liked to wear with the jacket, tied around the hanger as well. The scarf had a big dirty mark on it. We all tried his uniform on and marched up and down in front of the mirror, except Baghead who was too fat to fit into it. He just tried the cap on. The inside of his cap was covered in a white, flaky powder from all the gel Kingo's da wore. Chuckie asked where his gun was. We all had a good look, but we couldn't find it, which was just as well, because while we were looking we heard him try to get his key into the door. We could hear him struggling to get the key in. We all ran downstairs and pretended we were watching TV. Baghead just made it in time. Kingo's da had a big home entertainments centre which dominated one side of the front room. We got the TV on just in time. The screen was massive. It was like the pictures. Kingo told us he even had a TV in his bedroom. We all sat there staring at the television as Kingo's da shuffled in silence past us and went straight to bed.

Kingo's da came up to us outside the chip shop. We all said hello to him.

'How's it goin', lads?' he said. His breath smelt heavily of drink. Not sweet drink, like sherry, it was a heavier smell. 'Do you mind if I join you?' He took a sharp deep breath as if he was by the sea, breathing in the ozone freshness, the goodness of the sea air.

'This brings me back. Greasy Joe's chippy. Happy days. Pie and chips, fish and chips, scallop and chips, pastie and chips, sausage and chips, pie and chips. Fanta, Coke, Seven-Up. Pepsi. You name it, Greasy Joe's had it. The best chips and pasties in Belfast.'

He pulled out a packet of cigarettes and tapped the packet on the heel of his left hand. My eyes were drawn to this large gold ring on the fourth finger of his right hand. It looked like a horse's head. He saw me looking at it.

'Arkle,' he said. 'One of the greatest racehorses of all time.'

He held out the ring for me to appreciate its beauty, the horse's fine features captured for posterity on a ring with a clearly visible dent in it. It looked as if he might have punched a wall with that hand. Then slowly he displayed the ring to the rest of the boys. 'This ring cost me a bob or two. But I look on it as an investment, as an heirloom, something to leave my lads when I'm dead and gone,' he said.

'And wait until you see this.' He unbuttoned his shirt. He was wearing a gold chain with another horse's head on it. This horse looked nothing like the other one.

'Is that Arkle's cousin Sparkle?' said Chuckie.

Kingo's da threw him this look, a look which I thought was quite funny at the time. A half-composed look that took some time to assemble and therefore was really nothing of any substance, not real in any way. A joke. But Chuckie didn't seem to think that. 'Only kidding you, Mr King. I bet that's Arkle later in life after its racing days were over,' said Chuckie, backtracking.

'No, it's Arkle again at the height of his powers,' said Kingo's da. 'It's just from a different angle. Are you lads fucking stupid or what?'

'But it's nothing like the other one,' I said. 'It doesn't look anything like it.'

I thought Kingo's da was enjoying the crack. I thought he might appreciate a bit of banter. But I could tell immediately that I had misjudged his mood. He looked at me as if he was slightly puzzled by my audacity, as if he was slowly pondering what to do next, as if he was considering exactly where to land the punch. The cigarettes in his right hand probably saved me.

He sniffed loudly and turned away.

'Ignorant wee shites,' he said.

Slowly and carefully he offered the fags around. Chuckie, Tom and Jackie accepted a cigarette. I declined.

'What's the matter? Don't you smoke? Or is it that you just won't accept one of my cigarettes?' He looked around at the rest of them for backing. They were all standing there waiting for a light for their free smokes, all nodding back at him, as if he had just made some important point. 'Are you in training for something?' he said. 'A lot of footballers smoke. Do you know that? Georgie Best liked a fag when he was at the peak of his career, and it didn't do him any harm. He still managed to score a lot of goals.

'And a lot of women,' he added after a moment's pause.

He furrowed his brow, his eyes narrowing, staring straight at me. He leant towards me, fixing me with his look, and breathed out in my face. I wanted to turn my face to one side to avoid breathing in his fumes, but I kept my face in position, merely dropping my eyes to avoid returning his gaze from inches away. That's what he really wanted. Me breaking the stare, me giving in.

'Or are my cigarettes not good enough for you? He probably only smokes Silk Cut,' he said, turning now to the rest of the group. He was starting to smile, beginning to enjoy himself at my expense. 'Silk Cut is for queers, for puffs. You know that, don't you?'

I would have loved to have cracked him right in the kisser, to knock that big self-satisfied look right off his fucking face. But I had to keep that thought to myself, just in case he detected a fragment of it filtering to the surface. That would be very dangerous. Kingo's da was one of the top men in the Organization, so Kingo said. He knew everybody. And Kingo would always tell us that his da's favourite expression was 'It's not the dog in the fight that's important, it's the fight in the dog.' Baghead always found this very profound. But I sometimes wondered what fight there was in this person in front of me. When I was feeling brave that is.

He leant back again. He rubbed his hands over his protruding gut, like a fat man in anticipation of food. It looked odd, because in reality he was a skinny man, apart from that beer gut which looked as if it had been tacked on, as if it didn't quite belong. I imagined that his legs would be very thin and very white. Every time he annoyed me I imagined giving him a crack in the bake, and those thin white legs giving way, unable to support that unnatural weight piled on top.

'What will I have tonight? It's Tuesday, I think I'll have a pastie tonight. A big fat fuckin' pastie.' We all nodded, myself included, as if to applaud his decision-making.

'The pasties are lovely, Mr King,' said Chuckie. 'Absolutely brilliant.'

Kingo's da took a long pull on his cigarette. There was a sharp pop, as he let out the smoke.

'Can you blow smoke rings?' asked Chuckie.

'Blow smoke rings? I fucking well invented them,' said Kingo's da, as he emitted some vague outlines of rings into the October air. 'It's not the same since Greasy Joe retired, though,' he said. 'This new fella's pasties just aren't the same. I just can't get used to them. He's been here two years and I still can't get used to his pasties.'

'That's right,' said Chuckie, 'there's no two ways that they're as good as Greasy Joe's pasties. Greasy Joe's were out of this world.'

'Whatever happened to Greasy Joe?' I asked.

Kingo's da pulled himself upright with a good deal of effort.

'I'll tell you what happened to him. He said that he was fed up with all the intimidation around here. All the rackets. The protection money and what-have-you. So he packed it in. I think personally that he was just looking for an excuse to put his feet up. What do you think, lads?'

And we all nodded, although I was still thinking about giving him a dig in the face.

'Some people think they can pull the wool over your eyes, lads, but don't let them. It's a pity he's not here any more though. I miss Greasy Joe, even if he did try it on.'

I could see him looking at me again, targeting me. I tried not to catch his eye.

'You're Margaret Lyttle's son, aren't you? I knew your mother very well, and your da. He was a good man.'

I nodded. Lyttle was my mother's maiden name, but quite a few local people still used that name.

'Is your mother still up in the mill?' he asked.

'It's not really the mill any more. It's a thread factory now actually. It's not the way it was,' I said.

'What do you mean that it's not the mill any more? It'll always be the mill to me,' he said with some annoyance in his voice. He took a big pull on his cigarette to calm himself down. '"It's a thread factory actually."' He was imitating my voice. Chuckie and Jackie both laughed.

'You think you're something, don't you, because you went to that big fancy fucking school with the school uniform? You're a bit of a fucking snob if you ask me. Correct me if I'm wrong but you were expelled for cheating, isn't that right?'

I was going to say, 'Not exactly,' but I thought better of it.

'You're no better than anybody else around here. We've all cheated, you know. Any fucker can cheat. But some of us have a bit more intelligence to avoid getting caught. You couldn't even cheat right. You may have passed the Eleven Plus, but you probably cheated there as well.'

He looked around at the rest of them for approval. They were all nodding and grinning, anything to keep in with Big

Philip King, the big man in the Organization. He hadn't finished with me.

'No, I forgot. You haven't the intelligence to cheat properly. They probably marked your papers wrong. Or your answers got mixed up with somebody else's. Probably my son's in fact. You and him did the Eleven Plus at the same time. It was probably him who passed. He should have gone to that school not you. You cheated my family.'

He was managing to get himself worked up. I kept my eyes on him, just in case he made a swing for me. But I didn't look him directly in the eye. I looked downwards, but at an angle so that I could still watch him. Furrows had appeared on his forehead. Long deep angry grooves. I noticed that his eyes were bloodshot.

It was Chuckie who got me out of it. 'What was the mill like, Mr King?'

His expression started to change. For one of the top dogs in the Organization, he was easily distracted.

'That's a story and a half. I started my working life up there. Up there in the mill. I bet you didn't know that. I worked there for nearly two years. I hated the work. It gave me asthma. All that dust in the air. That's no condition for a young man. Mind you I was smoking forty a day at seventeen.'

And he burst out into a big, choking laugh, that had him bent double coughing and spluttering on the pavement. We all looked at each other. Chuckie bent down to check that he was all right.

'Are you all right, Mr King?'

Kingo's da straightened himself up. His face was a dangerous colour of red, and there was some spit resting on his lower lip. 'They were the days. The women who worked there got up to all sorts of tricks, and for a young lad that can be very flattering. I remember smart baaaalicks's mother, and big Dolores Adams. That's who she used to knock about

74

with in them days. Dolores was from that republican hole up there. You didn't worry in them days about what religion anybody was. I had a pal called Poker who was a Taig, who went to St Peter's, and he used to come down to our school to get me out of class. He'd come down and say Mr White wants to see Philip King. Then I'd go to my pal Rodney Smith's class and get him out of class, then we'd get Horsebreath Stephens out. It didn't matter in them days – Protestants and Catholics. We all messed about together. The Troubles changed all that. I don't know what happened to Poker in the end. Or big Dolores Adams. I don't even know if she's still a big girl. She's probably still wearing those same red knicks though. I bet she's still wearing the same panties.'

'She's probably still a big fat cunt,' said Chuckie.

Kingo's da didn't hear what he said, which I thought was probably just as well, because from his fixed faraway expression he was reliving happy moments, happy fragments, from long ago.

'Happy days,' he said. 'Happy days.'

His expression soon changed. 'She's probably married to some republican hood now,' he said, 'and living up West Belfast with him with a brood of wee Fenian kids running around the place. I probably wouldn't recognize her.'

He fished in his pocket, and waved Chuckie over.

'Here, son. Get me a pastie and chips. Keep the change.'

Chuckie took the two pound coins, and went up into the chip shop. He threw us a look which said, Mr Generosity, a pastie and chips costs one pound eighty, and he tells me to keep the change. I was relieved that Kingo's da did not spot his backward glance. We stood there in a quiet row, as if Kingo's da was one of us. It was funny to watch the locals go by all acknowledging him. We sometimes stood there for hours, and we could be invisible for all anybody cared. Until we said something that is, until we got into trouble. But

Kingo's da stood there, in the middle of our little group and everybody noticed him.

I saw Mrs Hutcheson walk along the pavement. She had her slippers on and a pint of milk in her hands. A coat pulled around her shoulders. She never said hello to anybody, but she gave him a lovely smile. I had never seen her smile before. It transformed her face. She always looked so cold; my mother had told me that her husband had been away for a very long time indeed, and that she was finding it hard.

I remember his name on the biggest wall mural in our neighbourhood. SOME GAVE THEIR LIFE, SOME SERVED LIFE. ALWAYS REMEMBERED AND NEVER FORGOTTEN. Johnny Hutcheson's name was up there: JOHNNY HUTCH – LIFE, crammed into a little box on one spoke of a huge array. Johnny Hutch is all that they ever called him, and it was shorter for the artist trying to represent years of fallen and captured comrades on the gable wall at the end of our street. But his name and all the others had been covered years ago by a billboard. Now the mural was concealed by a Wonderbra advert. *Hello boys,* it read.

'Hello, Philip,' she said. 'Are you trying to recapture your youth?' Her voice wasn't at all how I expected it to be. I had only heard her speak once before, and that's when she shouted at us for climbing along her yard wall. She sounded different tonight. She pulled her coat tight around her shoulders.

'You've caught me in my slippers. You don't expect to bump into anybody at this time of the night.' She glanced at the rest of us. We obviously didn't count, standing there in those twilight hours between the shops and the bookie's shutting and the bars opening.

'Hello, Linda. How are you? How's that husband of yours keeping? How's Johnny bearing up?'

It was a friendly sort of greeting. More than friendly. But I couldn't put my finger on why I thought so.

Chuckie came out of the chip shop with the pastie and chips. He handed the big greasy parcel to Kingo's da, and pointedly the twenty-pence coin. Kingo's da cradled the pastie supper in his hands, the coin trapped between the thumb and forefinger of his right hand.

'It's my supper,' he said. He kept it wrapped up. The two of them stood there not saying anything. They looked embarrassed because we were all stood there, gawking. I could see the grease stain spreading through the chip wrapper. Chuckie nudged me. I thought for a second that Kingo's da might toss the package away and make a run for it. He looked as if he had been caught red-handed doing something.

'I'd better let you get home then, and enjoy your tea,' said Mrs Hutcheson.

Kingo's da gave a faint, put-on smile. He looked relieved.

'I've been standing here gassing, giving these lads some advice. It was time I was off.'

He passed the pastie supper to his left hand and tucked it under his arm, the way you might hold a newspaper on the way to the office.

'See ya, lads,' he said. He gave her a bigger smile but it was still put on. His eyes didn't join in, they looked almost inquisitive, as if he was worried about what she might say next. He didn't say anything, then turned towards home. He seemed to have sobered up very quickly. He walked quickly away.

Mrs Hutcheson watched him for a few paces and then looked at us. She didn't speak, or even try to give us a half-smile. Then she set off in the opposite direction towards her empty house with the yard wall with the loose bricks, and a dog called Dinky that was always scratching itself.

'Do you think old Kingo's da's shafting her?' said Chuckie, as he watched her shuffle off in her slippers, the staccato movement making her big arse stick right out. 'Because I'd shag it.'

'Johnny Hutch would go fucking berserk if he was,' said Jackie. 'He's a wild man.'

'He's a wild imprisoned man,' I said. And we left it at that.

5

On Wednesday mornings the routine was different. We had steak on Wednesday. It was the big luxury of the week. A half-pound of steak for grilling, and a bone for Mrs Henderson's dog, Keeper. Keeper lived three doors away, and Mrs Henderson had Parkinson's disease, so she couldn't look after him too well. I used to take him for walks, and give him a bone every Wednesday. Keeper was half Alsatian and half collie, or near enough, and he used to follow me to school. Everybody thought he was my dog, but he wasn't.

One night when I tried to take him back home, Mrs Henderson had already gone to bed, so I had to put Keeper in our back room all night, but he scratched and howled until I let him out. I had to knock Mrs Henderson up in the middle of the night in order to get Keeper settled. I felt embarrassed whenever people called him my dog, because he wouldn't even stay in our house for one night.

Mrs Henderson had two sons, but they rarely came to visit. One had moved away to the other side of town. He had bought her this little mongrel pup to keep her company. The little furry pup with the brown patch on his chest turned into Keeper, who roamed the street as if he owned it, dragging discarded tyres with him wherever he went. I was the only person who could get the tyres off him, apart from Mrs Henderson, but she could never catch him. When the branches and the orange boxes and the tyres were collected every June and early July for the eleventh night, Keeper could be seen wandering around the streets, dragging a large branch or a tyre with him. None of the lads guarding the bonfire was brave enough to try to stop him helping himself to any tyre he wanted, or pishing on the bonfire whenever he felt like it. Our bonfire always reeked of Keeper's acrid scent. It was hard to make little huts in the jumble of branches to sit guarding the growing mountain of wood and rubber because of this smell.

Mrs Henderson's son had suggested calling the little pup Patch, and he was called Patch for his first three months, but after that he became Keeper, when Mrs Henderson's next-door neighbour Bertie Walmsley identified the maturing animal as a pedigree Alsatian, which quite clearly it was not.

Mrs Henderson's other son had gone to Canada. He only came back home once, but he looked alarmed when he saw what his mother was sharing a house with. He called up to our house, keen to show us all how he had broadened his horizons, how he had been changed by his new life across the ocean. I remember him asking, 'Can I use your washroom?' When he went up the stairs, my mother said, 'I've heard it called the shit house before, but never the washroom.' When he came back down, my mother tried to make a joke of it. 'I thought you were going to ask me, "Is your yard upstairs?"' He didn't laugh. I don't think he had much of a sense of humour. He didn't laugh when Keeper cocked his leg against him. He was busy telling my mother and me that his drive in Toronto was bigger than our street. I always knew Keeper was a very clever dog.

I went into the butcher's at about twelve o'clock. There was a queue as always. I slotted in at the back. All the coffin dodgers as Chuckie calls them, nattering away about nothing in particular. Two old women were talking about a programme that they had seen the previous night about Gulf War Syndrome. The programme had given out a number for those who needed help. It turned out to be a Kentucky Fried Chicken number.

'There were all these people ringing this number and talking about their problems, and it was just a Kentucky Fried Chicken number. This wee shite from the Kentucky place listened to all their problems, then asked them if they wanted any fries with that.'

Her friend was shaking her head. 'They've no respect the young people of today. None.'

'The problem is they don't know their arse from their elbow.'

'They've never had to work,' said her friend.

'They don't know what work is.'

They both looked at me, standing there with three pound coins in my hand. In their day I'd have been a veteran of the mill at my age. I'd have probably made it to the carding room by now. And here I was like a child out doing the messages for his mother.

A younger woman, who was standing just in front of them, started telling them about an incident down the road.

'Did you hear what happened the other night down there in Dover Street? The police came up and did raids on two houses. After they raided the houses they hung about. Then they started whistling the Irish National Anthem, and they were shouting, "Up the IRA." They were doing this just to wind the loyalist people up,' she said.

The two older women were going, 'Could you believe it?'

'Anyway,' said the younger woman with the bright blond hair, 'this child turned round and said to one of the policemen, "Mister, there's a banger at your foot." The policeman told the child to – pardon my language – "fuck away off" but the next minute, *bang!*, the banger went off, but the policeman wouldn't believe the wee child, and that wee child had tried to tell him. The policeman just said to him, "Aye, and there's one behind you. Fuck away off you wee shite." That's the way the RUC talk these days. It's all F-this and F-that all the fucking time, and that's the RUC for you, the *Royal* Ulster Constabulary.'

'The RUC isn't what it was,' said one of the older women. 'I wouldn't even say most of them are Protestant any more. I don't believe the statistics.' Her elderly friend was nodding. 'It's not a Protestant force any longer,' she continued. 'Most of them live in Protestant areas, but that doesn't mean that they are Protestant. I just think they feel safer in Protestant areas. That's why they live there. You can tell by looking at some of them that they're not Protestants. They look like Taigs. You can't fool me. You can always tell. Even in their uniforms, you can tell.'

It was the younger woman's turn again. 'The police came and arrested my husband about two years ago,' she said. 'Somebody had hijacked a lorry carrying electrical goods. They came and they searched our house. Somebody told them that my Bobby was involved in it. They told us what they were looking for – fridge-freezers, microwaves and electrical appliances, and anything like hoods or balaclavas or baseball bats. They turned the house over. My wee son Jamie had a baseball cap, which said *Belfast Children's Choir* on it. So they took this as evidence and arrested my Bobby. So Bobby says to them, 'Do you think that I'm going to go outside with a hat that says Belfast Children's Choir on it?' But this was their evidence and they put it in a wee bag. So they arrested him and they took him to Castlereagh. The things they told him in there were unbelievable. They told him that I was a whore, out whoring at nights and that I'd had a load of different fellas in the house. A different fella every night. Sometimes six fellas a night. The next day they told him a different story saying that I was arrested and the children were in care.'

'That's torture,' said one of the older women. 'You could go to the European Court of Human Rights over that.'

'That's right,' said the other old woman. 'That's mental torture. That's even worse than getting electric shocks on your privates.'

'Exactly,' said the blonde. 'And then there was this woman, a police officer, who was involved in the whole thing. My Bobby pointed her out down the town one day. She came in when they were interrogating my Bobby in Castlereagh with her wee skirts on and sat in front of him with her legs open, you know, flashing away. They were just trying to antagonize him, to get him going. That was just a wee thing that they did to Bobby, but they do even worse things than that there to some of the other Protestants. The Catholics make all the complaints, but we get treated worse. They don't get that type of treatment.'

'I know they don't,' said one of the older women. 'They reserve that treatment for us and our kind.'

Keeper kept popping his head around the door every time one of the coffin dodgers went in or out. He was panting away, his tongue lolling about inside his cavernous wet mouth. He was distracting me. I was enjoying listening to their stories. One or two of the old women tried to shoo him away, but he ignored them.

I had just turned round to look for Keeper when in walked one of the lads from the corner, Tony Tucker, and just behind him was Kingo's da. If we had been a proper gang, rather than a shifting collection of individuals with time on our hands, corner boys my ma called us, Tucker would have been the leader. Tucker was heavily built, 'well-made' my mother always said. He was two years older than me, and he worked as a labourer on a building site for some new flats off Springhill Street. His father got him the job. Tucker always liked to point out that these sorts of connections can come in very handy.

I remember when I was fourteen sitting up the glen one wet afternoon with Tucker and the lads. We had talked about turning ourselves into a proper gang, with initiation tests and codes of conduct, even codes of silence punishable by death. I had suggested that getting a tyre off Keeper might be one possible initiation ritual. But our plans hadn't come to anything. Tucker said that you couldn't just make up the rules for a gang, that's not how these things worked. These rules had to have been about for years, they had to evolve gradually to have any meaning.

And I remember thinking then that he was the natural leader, everybody listened to him, even though up to that point the rest of us had all been very keen on a gang with a brand-new code of conduct thought up on the spur of the moment. The next minute, he came up with an initiation rite all by himself that only he could do. It involved jumping off this twelve-foot drop up the glen on to a ledge at the side of a river, with barbed wire covering two-thirds of the ledge. He jumped first, Chuckie and Hammerhead hesitated. Hammerhead said that he had the wrong trainers on that day for such a jump. Then Tucker, to everyone's relief, said gangs were a load of shite anyway, and that the jump proved nothing.

When Mrs Henderson's son passed us all at the chip shop one night when he was over, he stopped to tell us about the sports car he happened to drive back home in Canada. Hammerhead asked him if he knew what they said about men who drive big, long sports cars. Mrs Henderson's son shook his head. 'They've got small dicks.' So Mrs Henderson's son told us that Toronto was full of proper gangs who had proper fights, not like the little scraps we got involved in. We knew they were little scraps, we called them skirmishes. So we never talked about gangs again, at least not in front of people.

But if we had we would have elected Tucker the leader.

Tucker could kick a guy in the face by hopping up on his back foot and throwing first his left foot and then his right foot in quick succession. To intimidate people he had just met, he would sometimes demonstrate this, stopping inches from their nose. He wore special shoes with a sharp metal horseshoe-shaped guard beneath the toecap. The horseshoe left a small semi-circular cut in the face. He told the shoe repairman that he needed the guard to stop him wearing down the soles of his shoes. He always said that he was very heavy on his feet. Tucker's acrobatic kick was usually enough to start off one of our skirmishes.

The day Mrs Henderson's son got a taxi back to the airport, he had a black eye. He said that somebody had kicked him in the face in the entry, but that it had been too dark to recognize who it was. We all had a good laugh at that, and at the little crescent-shaped cut beneath his left eye.

But I had never seen Tucker out with Kingo's da before. The two of them walked right to the front of the queue. They didn't notice me at first.

Mr Baxter, the butcher, greeted them. It wasn't a warm greeting, far from it, but he was trying desperately to be friendly. He was trying very hard to coax his face into a smile. He slapped some pork chops down on the counter. The old woman that he was serving tutted.

'Hello, Philip, you're a bit early today.'

Kingo's da nudged Tucker in beside him.

'I see you've got Rosemary Tucker's son with you. Is he helping out or . . . ?'

Tucker stood there, trying to look relaxed, his hands cupped in front of him. He had made an effort to dress up. He had a white shirt and tie with his bomber jacket over the top. It was probably a school shirt from three years ago, it was too small and it bit into his bullish neck. It still had inkstains on the collar. It was a while since Tucker had touched a pen that could leak ink like that.

'Tony is helping me out,' said Kingo's da.

Mr Baxter stood there, his lips slightly parted, the merest hint of a tired, desperate, put-on smile.

'It doesn't seem that long ago when I used to chase that lad for knocking on my door and running off.'

Tucker's face lit up. 'You and old Ruby Donaghy. You always gave the best chases.'

The expression on Kingo's da's face changed momentarily, as if he had been distracted, as if he was annoyed at himself for being so unprofessional.

'That was then,' he said. 'Now he's a big lad. He's matured. He's come on a lot. He's helping me out now.'

Mr Baxter stood there in silence, looking at the lad that three years ago tormented him every night, by kicking his door and running off into the park. A big well-made oaf whose shirt collar was the wrong size. His eyes moved slowly from Tucker to Kingo's da.

'Do you want me to see to you now?' he asked.

Kingo's da nodded. 'We're under a lot of pressure at the moment. I'm afraid we can't call back,' he said. 'Unfortunately.'

'Right now? Right this instant?' said Mr Baxter, obviously very aware that the shop was full, even though it was full of people of no consequence, like myself.

Kingo's da nodded again. It was as if he was trying to reassure him, and trying to hurry him along at the same time.

'I'm afraid so,' said Kingo's da.

I had never heard him be so polite before. He was obviously on the make.

Mr Baxter turned and went to the till. He had his back to me, and he tried to do it carefully and secretly, but I could still see him pull out five twenty-pound notes. He slipped them inside a brown envelope, which he had sitting ready beside the till. He handed the envelope to Kingo's da.

Kingo's da thanked him and then pointedly handed the envelope to Tucker, who put it immediately into the inside pocket of his bomber jacket.

'We have to get them used to responsibilities when they're young,' said Kingo's da. 'We'll see you next week but at the normal time. I'm sorry that we were a bit early this week, but the schedule's all out because I'm taking Tony around with me.'

And the two of them turned to go out.

I stepped out of the queue, right in their way. 'Tucker. How's about ye?'

For a second Tucker looked embarrassed, whether it was because of my friendly greeting, a friendly greeting from a lad obviously out doing the messages for his mother, or because of what had just transpired, I couldn't tell.

He blushed. I had known Tucker all my life, and I had never seen him blush like that before. I had seen him flushed with excitement, flushed with all his exertion in a skirmish, but I had never seen him show a natural, spontaneous, embarrassed blush. Kingo's da threw me a very thin nod, and mumbled something, then ushered Tucker out of the shop.

Mr Baxter was busy wrapping up the pork chops. He felt that he needed to comment on the little spectacle that a whole shop had witnessed.

'I had some work done on my house. Mrs Tucker's son did most of the heavy work. But Philip King was with him, grafting away, keeping an eye on things.'

And the two old women at the front of the queue just stood there with their arms folded, with a look that said, Everybody knows that Philip King has never grafted a day in his whole life.

I just couldn't stop smiling, thinking about Tucker coming of age. One of us out making it big on the street, and then, of course, there was the matter of the big, thick envelope in Tucker's inside pocket. This made me smile a whole lot more.

6

That night I got down to the corner early. I had a lot to tell the lads. None of them believed it.

'Tucker in the Organization?' said Hammerhead. 'Which? The UDA or the UVF? UDA. Baaaalicks. He's too much of a renegade for either organization. They'd never be able to control him.'

But I told them all that with my very own eyes I'd seen it all. Tucker and Kingo's da, and old Mr Baxter nearly choking as he handed Tucker the money.

Wee Bertie Smalls was transfixed. 'What was old Baxter's face like again? He's always been a mean auld bastard. It must have broke his fucking heart to hand over all those crispy notes.'

And we all stood there laughing. Wee Bertie had been down to Budget Drink for a couple of halves of lager for his da. Despite all their technology and the wee woman with the frizzy grey hair and the sharp little bird-like eyes behind the counter, he had still managed to lift a litre bottle of Bulgarian red. He had a technique, he always liked to tell us, but he would never disclose what this technique was in case one of us tried to copy it and was caught.

We would spend hours at the corner with wee Bertie going on about his fool-proof technique, and how one day he might, he just might let us in on it. I couldn't imagine how he managed it, but it must have had something to do with a blind spot in the shop, because everything he lifted seemed to come from the same shelf – Bulgarian red, Hungarian red with a big bull's face on the front, and once a big one-and-a-half-litre bottle of Coke, which I happened to notice was temporarily stored on the same set of shelves as the unpronounceable and virtually undrinkable foreign red wines.

The first mouthful was always disgusting, but after that it went down OK. We stood in a row passing the bottle carefully behind our backs, shielding it. When it was your turn you pretended to cough, bent yourself double then took a swig. By the time it got to my second turn, the coughs were more and more exaggerated. Mine was now a great hacking cough that had me spluttering and hacking on the pavement. The wine wasn't sour any more, but the bottle tasted of Hammerhead and old chip fat. I gulped at the wine as I pretended to cough, bent low on the wet greasy pavement. When I resurfaced I felt light-headed.

Then I saw him out of the corner of my eye. A right dander on him, swinging his shoulders, head back. The fella in the big picture, as my mother says. She had spent a lot of time at the pictures. I sat the bottle down on the pavement. For a second, I thought we were all going to break out into spontaneous applause.

'Act normal,' said Hammerhead. 'For fuck's sake act normal.'

Tucker came up to the end of the line as if nothing had happened, as if this was just another wet Wednesday night.

'Give us a drink of that there stuff,' he said. He took the bottle and took three big slugs. The rule was one slug at a time. Nobody tried to snatch the bottle off him. This was unusual. Then he held the bottle out in front of him and burped right down the neck. 'What kind of drink is this? It's fucking rotten.'

Chuckie was grinning. 'Only the best for you now,' he said.

'Champagne, Asti spumante, Smirnoff vodka, Black Bush, Martini.'

'You'll be buying up Budget Drink now,' said Bertie.

Tucker glanced my way. Not in a malevolent sort of way, just by way of registering that he knew that I had already spilt the beans. He leaked a little self-satisfied smile. He opened his leather jacket, and pulled out his wallet. We all crowded in around him.

'Give me air, for fuck's sake, give me a bit of space.'

He pulled out two ten-pound notes. I remember feeling a little disappointed. Just two dirty notes. I had expected sharp clean notes that might cut your finger as you flicked through them, not soiled wilted ones that drooped from your hand. But then I remembered it was only Wednesday. It was still early in the week. Tucker held up the drooping notes in front of him, and kissed them one at a time. It was then that the cheer went up. Even Hammerhead had lost control.

'You jammy fucking bastard. You lucky fucking cunt,' he said.

Tucker let go of the two notes and they fluttered for a few seconds in the damp air, before falling wearily to the pavement. The rest of us ran around after them, like children chasing bubbles. Then we started snatching them out of each other's hands and fighting for them. We were making a lot of noise. Even the woman behind the counter in Greasy Joe's came out to see what the matter was. I stuffed one of the notes into the back pocket of my jeans. I couldn't see who had pocketed the other one. I wasn't sure whether Tucker had intended to give the money away, but just in case he had I made sure that I got hold of some of it.

Tucker stood drinking from the bottle, his head thrown right back. The cheap red wine glug-glugging down his hard, muscular neck. His Adam's apple bobbed up and down like a float on a river. He drained the bottle, dregs and all, and sat it down carefully by the wall of the chip shop. It was as if the money had been forgotten about.

Tucker leant back against the chip shop. We all leant back with him, in a silent self-satisfied row. All happy and contented with our lot on easy street. This was only the start. Everybody knew there were plenty of perks for those who knew the right people. At last we were in on it. A bus went by with two lads we didn't know on the back seat. Two Fenian-looking wee bastards. They must have been Taigs, we knew where they were going. Tucker gave them the fingers. But with a smile on his face. They gave us the fingers back; one pulled down his pants and stuck his arse out the back window.

Tucker stood there grinning. Normally he'd have run after the bus, and dragged them off it. But tonight was no ordinary night. 'Leave them, lads, leave them,' he said magnanimously.

His voice had added authority.

Chuckie started to tell a joke. 'What do girls and Kentucky Fried Chicken have in common?' he asked. We all liked his jokes. He never forgot the punchline, unlike Baghead who always managed to get anxious before the end. 'After you've finished with the breast and legs you just stick your bone in a greasy box,' said Chuckie.

We were all laughing. One minute Tucker was looking as if he was enjoying himself with the rest of us, the next he was looking a bit agitated.

'By the way, lads, I want that money back. I was only messing about with it.'

But Chuckie just told him to shut up while he told his next joke. 'What do girls and dog shit have in common?' he asked. Chuckie was a great joke teller. He had one of those funny faces. 'They're both easier to pick up as they get older.'

Tucker waited patiently for Chuckie to finish. Then he

cut right in on the laughing itself. 'Right, lads, the kids' games are over. Hand them back,' he said, extending his left arm in the direction of nobody in particular. Nobody moved.

'I'm not fucking messing about here. The fun's over.'

I dipped my fingers into my pocket and pulled out the wilted torn note. I straightened it out, and was wetting the edges of the tear with spit to glue it back together, when Tucker snatched it from me.

'Right, the other one.'

I tried to smile, but the muscles around my jaw had gone hard. I squeezed and made a tight little grimace. I noticed that everybody else was grimacing as well.

Tucker stepped away from the wall, and looked slowly up the line, one by one. His eyes stopped at Hammerhead.

He extended his left arm again. Hammerhead looked down at it. Then the fingers crept forward.

'I don't know why you're looking at me,' said Hammerhead looking up. 'I never saw your fucking money. It's one of these other cunts.'

Tucker didn't break eye contact and he didn't blink. His fingers just splayed outwards. The motion caught Hammerhead's eye. He glanced down again. He looked as if he had something to hide. Even I thought that.

He made eye contact again with Tucker. 'I'm telling ya. I didn't touch your fucking money.' Hammerhead's voice was getting higher. He was whining.

'I'm going to search you,' said Tucker.

'You're going to what?' Hammerhead looked around at the rest of us with a look of incredulity. 'Like fuck you are.'

'Just give him his money,' I said. 'For fuck's sake let's stop this nonsense.'

'I haven't got his money. I never fucking touched it. But there's no way he's going to search me. No fucking way.' Hammerhead was shuffling in the one position, as if he was about to walk away but couldn't conjure up the necessary mental force to do it. He looked uneasy.

Tucker took a step back. I knew what it meant. Hammerhead must have known. But he didn't move now. He had gone quite still, like an animal dampening down its visceral responses to focus on the threats in the environment. Tucker suddenly hopped up on his back foot and lashed out with his feet. The timing was like the little end sequence at the end of one of Jimmy Tarbuck's jokes, or Basil Brush. That's it: Basil Brush. The sequence he uses just in case you haven't quite got it, just in case you haven't quite recognized that that's your lot.

Boom-boom. Exactly like that. *Boom-boom.* The same speed, the same timing. Just imagine saying it. It's as quick as that. Two feet in the face as quick as that. No gap between the blows landing on the bone in the face, one noise dying while the other one started. *Boom-boom.* Tucker was very quick with his feet. Everybody who has ever seen him in action would tell you that.

Hammerhead sank on to his knees cupping his hands around his nose, his nose spurting blood. He was whimpering into the little triangular echo chamber of his hands. It gave his voice a certain resonance.

'You've broken my fucking nose.'

He started sniffing loudly, as if he was trying to draw a breath.

Tucker stood over him, and started going through the pockets of his denim jacket. Hammerhead didn't try to stop him. I saw Chuckie pull a note out of his own pocket and let it fall gently to the ground. It was Chuckie who spotted the missing note lying in a puddle just by the air vent of Greasy Joe's.

Tucker didn't say anything. He just bent down and picked the note up. It was almost torn in half. He shook it once and stuffed it into the pocket of his jeans.

'Don't fucking mess with me,' he said, and strode off. Tom, Chuckie and wee Bertie made some lame excuse about having to be home early and ran after him, the four of them walked back home together. We could hear them laughing.

I helped Hammerhead up. Paul and Jackie just looked on. 'That's right, you two just stand there,' I said.

Paul just blew his breath audibly out and made an upturned-hand gesture, as if to say, What can you do?

Paul, Jackie, Hammerhead and myself stood there in silence. Hammerhead was still holding his nose with the palms of his hands.

'He always was a bit of a fucking Comanche,' said Paul. 'A bit of a wild man. But he's even worse now he's got all these connections. Who the fuck does he think he is?'

'I know who he is, he's a fucking dead man,' said Hammerhead. 'A fucking dead fucking man. If my cousin wasn't inside, do you think that he would have done this?'

We all shook our heads. Hammerhead's nose sounded blocked up. I was trying not to laugh.

I stood there thinking that a week ago we all said these things and it was all just show. It was just part of who we were. Wild threats were part of us, part of how we talked. But Tucker had done this in front of everybody.

Jackie said he'd got some chewing-gum remover at home, which was good for getting the bloodstains out of clothes. So he took Hammerhead home with him. Paul and I stood at the corner for another half an hour. Neither of us said anything. Paul lit up a cigarette, his last one. He crumpled up the packet, threw it up in the air and kicked it away. An RUC Land-Rover pulled up. We hadn't seen them coming. We were usually much more observant than that. They didn't say anything at first. They just sat there, parked on the road, watching us quietly. We tried to avoid looking at them. One of them sitting in the back pointed at the packet.

'Pick that up.'

Jackie and I stared back as if we didn't quite understand what was being asked of us, as if we didn't know anything about discarded cigarette packets lying on pavements.

'That's right, you on the right. Pick that up.'

Jackie walked along the pavement and lifted the crumpled packet. He stood there as if he was waiting for further instructions.

'Now put it in your pocket and fuck off home.'

We started to shuffle off home. We could see them sitting there waiting to see if we'd try to return. They were having a good laugh about something.

Suddenly, Jackie shouted: 'Up your hole with a big jam roll.' He was off before he got to 'roll'. I hadn't expected it. I was slow. The Land-Rover roared into life. It did a loud sharp U-turn. I ran across the road and up the street. I took the first entry and out at the top. Then I dived under the first car on the left. I lay there, breathing heavily. I could hear the deep roar of the Land-Rover up and down the street. There were boys my age being beaten on these streets with sticks with nails in them, and it was me and Jackie they were hunting, for shouting something that they probably couldn't even make out. I kept my face to the ground, to soften my breathing. I could smell the oil, and I thought of my father. It was always the same. Every time I was on the run, I'd hide under a car. That was my style. Some of the lads would try to leg it home. I would lie low and breathe in fumes from the tarmac and remember him. I was starting to associate him with fear. I stayed there until the police got bored.

My mother was sitting knitting when I got in. The TV was on, but the picture wasn't very good. The vertical control button was lying on the floor in front of the television. She had obviously given up on it. I found the *click-clack* of the knitting needles vaguely reassuring. It sounded very home-like. She was in a better mood. Our next-door neighbour had had a baby, so she said that she would knit something for it. She asked me what kind of night I'd had. I said not bad. I didn't mention Tucker's new line of work, or his skirmish with Hammerhead.

She had been tidying up and had rearranged some ornaments and some old photographs. The lucky leprechaun from Galway had been moved from the top of the stairs to the top of the television. Perhaps she thought it might do some good there. A picture of her and my father had been put in a new frame. The frame had been forced into a little wooden base from some broken ornament. It said *squirrel* on the front of it. She saw me looking at it.

'He was a good-looking man your da.'

I looked at his eyes and the brown striped suit he was wearing and tried to remember him dressed up like that, proud to be going out with my mother. But that was long before I was born. I could only remember him in overalls on winter's nights, when the eyes behind the glasses had dulled a little.

'And one of the politest men you would ever meet,' she said. 'He would never break wind in the house. He would always go out to the street for that.'

My eyes had shifted down to the inscription for *squirrel* on the base of the photograph. I was wondering if she hadn't noticed it.

'There were both men and women crying at his funeral. Did you know that? He was loved by everybody. Do you remember his funeral? Do you remember him being carried out of the street?'

I nodded quietly.

'When I die, I don't want to be carried like that. I'm afraid that they might drop me. I want to be buried from a funeral parlour, with no carrying. You will remember that, won't you?'

She was knitting away, pink fluffy wool billowing out from the needles.

'You miss him, don't you?'

It was rare for her to ask me this sort of question directly. The emotions were still too raw even after five years for both of us. We both liked to channel our emotions in other ways. Even anger was better than this.

She didn't let me answer. 'It just isn't fair. You look at all these no-good cowboys on the street, and it's your father who's been taken away. I heard that what's-his-name, the big Godfather, what do you call him? Anyway, he had all the streetlights down the road put out. He said that it was to stop snipers having a go at him or any of the residents. But he only did it to show that he was the big boss around here. If you wanted your light back on you had to go to see him to ask him personally to arrange for the light to be put on. He had Tommy Lee, who used to work for the electricity board, running up and down the road with a big ladder putting the lights back on. But only on his say-so. I heard that you had to pay him for the privilege. But you don't know whether that's true or not.' The needles were working away more frantically now. 'But we still need the Organization to protect us from the IRA and to keep the yahoos in check, like that wee shite the other night on the telly. The wee shite who got what was coming to him probably for selling drugs. That's what you get if you try to sell drugs here, you get the Organization calling round at your house and taking you out for a wee walk round the entry. The RUC are too soft, their arms are tied, but the Organization know what to do with yahoos. They know how to treat them.'

I went and got four Jacob's Cream Crackers and some cheese from the fridge and a pint of milk. I sat on the pouffe in front of the television, which was now making a loud humming sound.

'You're not going to drink out of that bottle, are you? Get a glass you lazy wee shite.'

I took a long deep slug from the bottle. She didn't seem to notice.

'Your father would never have been involved in anything like that, you know. He was too much of a gentleman. He used to fix your man's car for him. In all weathers he would be down the road lying below the big Godfather's car. I'm sure your man never got round to paying him.'

I could hear the needles clacking more forcefully against each other, as she thought about all the things that we might have had if fate had just been that much kinder. But I didn't want to talk about Kingo's da or Tucker or financial obligations in our small community. I didn't want to talk about emotion or heartache or long sleepless nights trying to recapture the sound of his voice. I didn't want to try to describe that burning chasm of loss, which opens up every morning and every night before conscious effort kicks in and you can control what you feel. I just wanted to say something about him, altogether less painful.

'I just wish he had got the chance to teach me to dive,' I said finally.

The needles stopped momentarily. She looked at me. 'That would have been difficult for him. He couldn't swim. That's why he never took you to the swimming baths. I know he was always promising you, but I thought you'd have realized when he never went that there must have been some reason for it.'

I sat there, and I could feel myself going numb. Numbed by all the events of the day, and by this. The worst shock of them all. I had told Tucker for all those years at primary school that my da was a champion swimmer and that one day I would dive like him.

'He couldn't swim?' I tried to say in a light-hearted way

with a nice light, chirpy melody, as if I hadn't a care in the world, but it came out full of stops and starts.

'I thought that your father could swim when I first met him,' said my mother. 'He had always told me he went regularly to Falls Road Baths but he just went to watch his mates. After we got married, we went down to Helen's Bay for the day. He got changed and ran down to the water's edge. He dipped his toe in and ran back. That man couldn't have dived to save his life.'

She was smiling. It was the first time in ages that I had seen her smile. I felt as if I couldn't move. 'It was lovely down in Helen's Bay on a good day,' she said.

The crackers dried in my mouth. I couldn't swallow the thick lumpy paste. I had to disgorge the last mouthful of chewed cracker on to the plate in front of me, but she didn't notice. She was knitting away, smiling at happy memories. The clack-clacking of the needles didn't sound reassuring now, but menacing. Hard metal on metal.

'Oh, by the way,' she said. 'Your friend Tony Tucker rang earlier. He's a nice lad, that. Very kind to his mother. He looks after her well, you know. He says that he wants to meet up with you tomorrow. He says that he may be able to put a little bit of work your way.'

She was knitting away, the pattern sitting on her knee. The pattern showed a bright chubby blond baby covered in thick pink chunky wool from head to toe.

'Perhaps a wee job has come up on that building site where he works,' she said. 'That would tide you over until you decide to go back to your studies. Perhaps our luck is in for once. Perhaps everything is going to change for the better.'

7

I was still in bed when Tucker arrived. I heard him letting himself in. I had been lying in bed thinking. He shouted up the stairs, then I could hear him trying to put the TV on. I heard him shout the first time, but I let him call up the stairs a few more times. I didn't want him to think I would just jump whenever he called.

He never got angry the way my mother did when I didn't answer immediately. When she got no response in the morning you could hear her ranting and raving, talking to herself. She took silence very personally.

I came down in my pyjama bottoms. He had got the TV to work and was helping himself to some cornflakes. I noticed that he had washed the bowl before using it. Some cookery programme was on the telly.

'You want to get this TV seen to. It's not working right,' he said. 'Where's the vertical-hold button, and I'll try to fix it for you.'

I told him that the vertical-hold button was about somewhere, but it had been getting a lot of use recently. He set down his cornflakes and got up from the settee. He walked over to the set and hit it somewhere near the top on the right-hand side.

'This always does the trick,' he said.

The picture went dead.

'Sorry about that,' he said. 'You want to give wee Joe a ring. He's very good with old sets like this one.'

I nodded wearily. Tucker sat down opposite me again and started once more on his cereal. He glanced across at me.

'Have you been playing with yourself in those pyjamas?' he said. 'They look a bit crusty to me. I bet your ma doesn't have to change your bed, I bet she just shuffles your sheets every morning.'

I yanked the front of the pyjama bottoms round, without looking down.

Tucker was laughing. 'I thought you'd spilt some milk of magnesia down the front of your pyjamas there for a while,' he said.

A heavy lorry rumbled past on the road outside. The thin walls of the house vibrated. The windowframes shook.

'Well, what about last night then?' he asked. He lifted his eyebrows expectantly and waited. I watched a large drip of milk fall on to his lap.

'Well not too good really,' I said. 'I don't think that fighting among ourselves is too clever. We've only got each other.'

'Not too good?' said Tucker. 'It was fucking brilliant. I've been waiting for a chance to deck Hammerhead. He can be a greasy wee cunt sometimes. I loved giving him a good kick in the gob.'

Tucker's face had a faraway look.

'How did it happen again?' he said. 'I just remember looking at him and knowing I was going to do it. I just knew it. I didn't move. Then my body started moving automatically, as if I wasn't controlling it.'

I just sat there, letting him enjoy his moment.

'The next thing I knew I could just see this blood spurting out of his nose, splashing all over the place. Over my shoes as well. I had to step right back to keep my shoes clean. His nose was making these little noises all by itself, these little squeaking noises, as if there was some animal trapped up there.'

Tucker was shaking his head and smiling, as he relived the fragments from the night before, the fragments he was sticking together.

'And what about yesterday afternoon?' he said. 'Me and Big Phil on my home turf? I loved going into old Baxter's. Did you see his face? He's always been a miserable auld bastard.'

Tucker was still smiling, still shaking his head, still looking very pleased with himself. He was lapping up the milk from the cornflakes. Suddenly he stopped. His mouth curled upwards, as if he had just been poisoned, which he clearly thought he had.

'Aaaaah. This milk's a bit fucking sour,' he said. 'I think it's fucking well gone off.'

He passed the bowl over to me. 'Does fucking nothing electrical work in this fucking house of yours?'

I snatched the bowl and stuck my nose right down into it, as close as I could to the tiny residue of milk left lying in the bottom of it. It smelt bad. I was amazed that he had managed to eat a whole bowl of flakes drenched in sour milk.

'It smells all right to me,' I said. 'You must have a bad smell in your nose.'

I got up and walked into the kitchen and dumped the plate into the sink. I walked over to the fridge and opened the door. Some ham half wrapped in tin foil was lying on the second shelf. Most of the stuff in the fridge was half covered in tin foil, as if nobody could really be bothered. I picked up the ham and smelt it. It was bad.

'The fridge is working OK,' I shouted into the next room. 'There's definitely something wrong with your sense of smell. You want to go the doctor's and get yourself seen to.'

Tucker ignored my comments. He had picked up the *News-letter*, the condensed version, the taster delivered free of charge to homes like ours in North Belfast. I had never seen him with a newspaper in his hand before. He was acting serious. It was as if he was searching for an item in the news to act as a cue so that he could unburden himself to me. Although in truth I felt that his new secrets weren't that much of a burden to him. He looked far too pleased with himself for that.

At last he found something that would do the trick. He found an item about a former UFF member being refused a visa to the United States. A former murderer, now conveniently born again, wanted to go to Texas to give his testimony. But he had been refused permission to enter the country.

'It would be fantastic to visit Texas at this time of the year,' he said. 'Imagine visiting the Alamo. This man's done his time and he's a Christian. What's the problem? I don't see any problem there. Do you?'

I said nothing, because I knew that he didn't want an argument. He just wanted my attention.

'I joined up four months ago,' he said quietly. 'The Organization,' he added. 'The UDA.'

He left a serious solemn pause. The house seemed very quiet. It was as if the traffic had been stopped for an instant.

'Oh,' I said.

'It was Big Phil who suggested it to me originally,' continued Tucker. 'He just came round to our house one night and just told my parents he wanted to talk to me in private. He came right out with it. He told me that it was time for me to do my bit for God and Ulster. My da was sitting there nodding away at everything Big Phil said. My da had been down in the bar all afternoon, he would have nodded at anything. Phil had to ask him to leave in the end. My ma went to make the tea. But she was listening from the other room. I could see her head popping around the door. I think she was under the impression that the UDA were after me for something and that Big Phil had come for a quiet word to warn me, sort of thing. She looked almost relieved when I told her afterwards what he was really after.

'Big Phil knew where I stood. He knew that I'm a loyalist. I'm not bitter, but I'm a loyalist through and through.'

Tucker was looking at me for reassurance that nobody could ever accuse him of being bitter. We'd had our skirmishes with Catholics over the years, but there was no bitterness in any of the violence. We just didn't like them. It was as simple as that. A few of the lads were bitter. Chuckie had been stabbed in the foot by one, and had to hijack a Ford Fiesta to take him to the Royal's casualty department. He was bitter after that, but only because everyone was laughing at him.

'There's no way that I'm bitter,' said Tucker. 'Sure we used to go to the Globe some Fridays. All the barmen there were Taigs. Every one of them. And your woman behind the bar was called Theresa. If I was bitter I wouldn't have drunk in that Fenian hole.'

I didn't remind Tucker that he ended up getting barred from the Globe for fighting with one of the barmen about some disputed change, and that the last time I saw its ornate stained-glass window there was a large hole in the middle of it, where Tucker had heaved a brick right through it.

'The way Big Phil put it was that even when things are a little quiet, do you think the IRA ever stop recruiting or getting ready for their next massacre?'

I was trying to agree with him, to make him feel better about his momentous decision. He had joined the UDA. We always said that we wouldn't get involved in anything like that, that once you're in, you're in, and there's no way out. We had talked about it a hundred times. Billy had always told us that he had been asked to join the UVF. He was the first to be asked from our gang. He said that the question

105

he got put to him was, 'Could you walk into a living room and see your target sitting there and just go for the hit? Say he was an IRA man, could you shoot him dead in front of his wee children?' Billy always said that his answer was that he couldn't do it in front of the man's family. So Billy told us that your man just said to him, 'Well then, we'll not talk to you any more about joining the UVF.'

Billy always liked to talk about the guys he had known from school who were now in the UVF. 'Some of my mates wouldn't give a fuck,' he'd say. 'They'd push the wee child out of the road and shoot him just to get at their target. That's how bad they are. But in other ways they're dead on. You can go out with them and have a good drink with them and a good laugh. They're probably only bitter because they've lost close family to the IRA. I'd only join the UVF if it came to civil war, to protect my kids. But not at the moment.'

We had always agreed with him, we had reached our decision. But that was all gone now. Tucker had been flattered that Big Phil had actually gone to his house to ask him personally to do his bit. Big Phil had asked Tony's da to leave the room. His da had never been asked to join. Tony was the man of the house now.

It was odd to sit there watching Tucker act so seriously. He had always been a joke a minute before. He was trying very hard to be different. I respected him for it.

'We can't let our defences down against the republican movement,' said Tucker. 'I've always thought that. But that's what Big Phil says as well. I listened to him that night, then I made up my own mind.'

Tucker set the newspaper down. 'But I couldn't talk about it down at the corner,' he said. 'I wanted to tell all the lads about it, but I was under orders not to discuss my new life in the Organization.'

'So here I am,' he said. He jumped back in his seat, as if

marking out a new dramatic phase in his young life. 'So far I've just been doing some collection work for the Loyalist Prisoners' Welfare Fund. They look after the families of the boys inside, you know. Phil tells me that Sam Smiley got a new car when he got out. His family had put all the money away for him. It all mounts up over seventeen years you know. He got a lovely wee silver car when he got out. It was a wee Nissan Micra. I think it may have had power steering, but I'm not sure about that.'

The name Smiley rang some vague bell. I had seen it on a gable wall somewhere. SMILEY – LIFE. Somebody had drawn a little smiley face by the side of it. That's probably why it stuck in my mind. If it wasn't for the smiley face I'd probably never have remembered it at all.

'What was he in for?' I asked.

'You mean to say you don't remember William Smiley? Wily Smiley they called him, because he was a cunning wee cunt. You must remember Wily Smiley. He did that wee murder in Brick Street. You remember your man was coming across from that Republican area and he slowed down on the ramps at Brick Street. You remember that surely? Everybody remembers that murder. He had his lad with him. You must remember the shooting of the wee lad? But nobody saw the wee lad sitting there. My ma told me that there was a big fuss about it at the time. The lad was crouched down in the passenger seat. Nobody saw him until it was too late. How could you see a wee lad crouched down like that in the front seat of a Ford Granada? Answer me that.'

'You couldn't,' I said.

'Exactly,' said Tucker.

'Anyway Wily Smiley was only the driver, he wasn't the gunman. There were two other men who actually did the shooting. But Smiley never turned into a supergrass. He kept his trap shut and went to the Maze and now he's got a lovely wee Nissan Micra with power steering. I saw him in it on the Shankill earlier this week. It's his pride and joy. He's out cleaning it every day. It's a lovely wee car, and he looks after it well.'

Tucker leant forward conspiratorially, until he was nearly falling off his seat. He was going to get more personal. You could tell. 'Big Phil has been taking me out with him for a few weeks,' he said. 'But yesterday was the first time up here, up in my own neighbourhood. I couldn't believe it when I bumped into you. I was quite pleased afterwards but not at the time.

'But then I had an idea when I went home. You're educated and you could use that education to help us out. You see we have to call at different times every week and sometimes businessmen aren't ready for us. It sometimes takes them a wee while to get their contributions together. So I thought that it would help to get these wee flyers printed telling them what time we're going to call. Then they'd be ready for us. We could pretend we're a window-cleaning business or something, and just give a date and a time when we're going to be there. I mentioned my idea to Big Phil and he thinks it's a great idea. He says I've got a lot of initiative. The only problem is that my spelling isn't too good. That's where you come in. You were always good at spelling at school, so I thought you could do it for me. That's why I'm here.'

I had tried to be the audience that Tucker wanted, but my control was weakening. At first I had caught myself smiling, but by the time he had finished I was laughing from my belly up.

'Are you fucking serious?' I said, the question elongated with great burps of laughter. 'Flyers? Fucking flyers?'

I was trying to get Tucker to laugh with me, but he sat with a resigned, slightly quizzical expression, as if he really didn't understand what I found so funny.

'Let me get this right. You want to publicize when you're going to call for protection money. Is that right?'

He nodded his head impatiently.

'You mean to say that you want to tell the police when and where you're going to be operating your racket in the community around here? Have you gone fucking crazy?'

'You've got the wrong end of the stick,' said Tucker. 'It's not a racket. Our lads have done their bit for Ulster. Their families need looking after. It's as simple as that. Old Baxter has done fuck all for Ulster, except give out a few free chops to families at Christmas, so he should pay up. He's getting off lightly. Some lads have given their life. Anyway it's all going to be in code. I'll see to that with your help.'

Tucker started fishing in his pocket and pulled out a single sheet of lined paper folded over twice. He passed it to me. He had written the heading in red capital letters. GLENVIEW CLEANING SERVICES. Then in blue capital letters he had DATE AND TIME OF YOUR NEXT APPOINTMENT.

'I want to add a bit about the service,' he said. 'Like an advertising jingle. "Glenview, the very best in town, top quality cleaning for bottom-of-the-range prices." That kind of thing. But I thought you might have a go at writing this for us. Big Phil would be very grateful. He'd also be very grateful if you kept an eye on the spelling. He says we don't want to look like mugs. We went down through a nationalist area a few days ago, and those cunts from down there had written on the wall, "Informers beter beware." Now even Big Phil knows that's not how you spell "better". But I think he looked the correct spelling up. He says it just makes them look stupid. It's not very professional. We want to do a better job, and create the right image.'

I watched an RUC patrol pull up outside the window. It was raining. I watched the tick-tock of the wipers as the

Land-Rover turned across the street. Three officers climbed wearily out of the back of the wagon. They were setting up a checkpoint for cars just outside the front door. It was strange to be able to study their features in this way, through glass, as if they were in a fish tank and you had all the time in the world just to watch their lazy movements and their vacant expressions. A drop of water crawled down the window. I watched it slink to the left. The RUC men stood in the same position.

'This is what we have to deal with,' said Tucker, pulling me over to the window. 'They're only human like us. Do you think that big fat bastard there with some big house up the other end of town really cares about what we get up to here, as long as we don't bother him? He's only worried about his overtime. That's all he cares about. This wee scheme won't hurt anybody. It's just to make sure that everybody does something.'

I watched the rain on the road. The uneven tarmac was filling with water. A dog sloped off home, carefully avoiding the puddles. It stopped every few seconds to shake itself. The sky was grey and low. It was a bad day to be out and those three men clearly resented having to stand on our road checking documents. They wanted to be somewhere else.

'Some people have to give a lot more,' said Tucker. 'Now that I'm involved I don't know what I'll be asked to give. But one thing's for sure . . .'

The rain was bouncing off the window. You could watch it ricochet off the peak caps of the RUC men.

'What's that?' I asked.

'Some fuckers around here will be asked to give more than they have been,' said Tucker. 'And I'm the boy to enforce it.'

I laughed quietly. I could see that Tucker had this unique opportunity to even a lot of old scores, even petty scores from childhood, and he wasn't going to let this opportunity pass him by.

Tucker pressed the sheet of paper into my hand. 'I'm meeting up with Phil on Saturday night,' he said. 'Make sure that you've got it done by then.'

He was just about to leave, when suddenly he noticed a fourth officer getting out of the van.

'I recognize that guy there. Isn't he that fella that clipped me that night about a year ago in Royal Avenue for giving him some cheek? Do you remember the night I stuck Jackie's head into the litter bin? This cunt turned up and started acting the fella in the big picture, ordering us around.'

I looked out through the glass, but the young officer had pulled his hat low to keep the rain off. I could only see part of his face. I said that I didn't recognize him.

'They all look alike to me,' I said. 'You have to be a clone to get into the RUC.'

'Well I do, so that's another one for my little black book.'

Tucker was grinning so widely that I assumed this was some sort of joke. But you should never jump to conclusions. My father used to say this. That's one thing I do remember from him.

'Have you got any exercise books from that school of yours handy to be my little black book?' asked Tucker. 'I better start writing some of these names down.' He was laughing away, pretending to lick a pencil and write some names down. 'There's Hammerhead, that cunt out there, Raymond Lloyd who owes me some money, what was that teacher called who was always getting the cane out when he wasn't supposed to?'

He sprang up out of his seat, still smiling, and went out into the rain.

'See you tomorrow,' he said. 'Get working.'

111

I watched him push past the young officer on the pavement who looked straight up at him.

I thought at the time that this was probably one of the stupidest things this young RUC officer had ever done.

8

Belfast is a neat little town crouching at the bottom of a horseshoe of hills. You can sit on the Cave Hill by Napoleon's Nose and view the whole thing lying there as if in the palm of somebody's hand, the town cradled by the arms gently holding it.

It was rare for Tucker to go for walks with me and the dog, but he could tell I was not convinced by all the changes in his life, by his involvement. He wanted me to understand his decision, he wanted us to be together on this, so we sat together in the wind, watching Belfast beneath us. Of course, he never said any of this but he didn't have to. I knew. As soon as he told me that he wanted to go out with me and the dog I knew.

I sat there with Keeper and Tucker that afternoon looking down at the Belfast beneath us and thinking, Is that all there is? We worked our way across town, up streets that we knew and down streets that we didn't know. Streets me and him would never walk. You could see how streets joined together from up there. I could see my school and its rugby pitch and way across town I could see the tight little lines of the mill houses and the outline of the mill itself. Just round the hill a bit I could see tight little rows of streets like ours but ones that meant nothing to me, streets that led nowhere. Fenian streets where we would never dare go.

Keeper sat beside me shaking slightly with exhaustion. He nearly caught a rabbit on the way up. He had chased the rabbit through the dank meadow of the glen, where the river works its way through from some buried source in the hill down to the railings of the school where it disappears into the earth again. The rabbit had found the tufts of grass above the stagnant earth; Keeper had gone right through the brackish pools, and lost him. The underside of his coat was covered in mud, the hairs were matted like dark feathers. He lay trying to clean himself, his hard muscular body rising and falling with the deep breaths.

I sat there thinking about Tucker's plan, and the slogan for Glenview Cleaning Services. All I could come up with was 'This wee town's biggest agency. We do the business on your doorstep'. I hoped Kingo's da had a sense of humour. I didn't mention it to Tucker just yet. I saved it until the walk down.

We waited until teatime and cut down through the glen down the side of the school. Fields of tall, dead nettles, turning brown. We cut their dead heads off with sticks we used as scythes. Keeper chased the flying heads. Down past the ripped parcels of refuse, where our neighbours had taken carrier bags of rubbish and dumped them in the fields nearest their homes. The stomach of the bags ripped open, spilling out their contents. Large mongrel dogs were out on their own, marking out their territory, watching us, barking after Keeper.

Two young boys were out asking for money for Hallowe'en. They were a bit early. One came up to us. Tucker said that he had no change. I gave one of the lads fifty pence, my last fifty pence, because I was feeling generous, and his friend hurried over.

'How much did you give him?' he asked.

'Tell him it was ten pence,' said the first, turning his back on his friend.

'Ten pence,' I said, and I walked on, not really understanding why I had decided to go along with this small deception.

One small boy cheating his friend on the street for half the proceeds. A chasm being carved between them for the sake of a few pence profit. There was a lot of that about our street.

The streets were quiet except for the dogs, and the small children. Home from school and told to play out until their tea was ready. We cut through the estate. Two small dirty boys were pushing an old pram full of stones along the pavement. One wore a red jumper with a yellow hoop, the other a red jumper that had been washed until it was nearly pink.

'There she is,' said one of them.

My eyes were drawn to a young blonde girl of about six on the other side of the road where the flats once had stood, before they were demolished. There used to be a drinking club in those flats, but I had never been in it. I was too young and one night some armed masked men came in to steal a gun off an off-duty UDR soldier having a drink in the shebeen. There was an exchange of gunfire and when the smoke cleared the uncle of one of my schoolfriends was left dying on the ground. It was never clear whether he had been one of the men in the masks or not. None of the witnesses ever agreed about what had happened. The judge at the trial said it was like something out of the Wild West. But after that the club was closed down, and the flats demolished. All that was left were lumps of concrete in piles that had collapsed, concrete weathered and charred by soot, and stories about who pulled their gun first, and who was the quickest on the draw with a pistol up our way. Tucker told me that his da used to go on about this guy's fantastic funeral, a full military funeral with all the trimmings.

The young boys tipped the stones out on to the pavement into a neat pile, and started firing them one at a time at the young girl, who never budged. She just swayed this way and that to avoid the stones. She looked defiantly at them. There

115

was certainly no fear in her eyes. Tucker looked amused.

'She's got some bottle,' he said.

'Wee bitch,' said the smaller of the two boys.

'Wee shites,' said the girl back; 'wait until I tell your mothers that you're picking on a wee girl. Pick on somebody your own size. You're a couple of wee cowards.'

She picked up a stone and hurled it at the boys. One of them tried to kick it. Then she picked up a half-brick. The boys started to move backwards, all the time watching her, leaving their neat pile of stones behind, like some ancient half-understood monument from an earlier time. They swore back at her, but they didn't return. She played with the stones they had thrown at her, as if they were a present. She made a tall pillar and then kicked it over.

Tucker told me that he wanted to call in to a friend of his sister's. He asked me if I remembered a shooting in a video shop a bit less than a year ago. His sister's friend was there that night. He thought it would do me good to meet her. We cut down the backs of the houses, and knocked on a back door. There was no answer. I could hear a child crying. The child interrupted its crying to shout to its mother.

'Mammy, Mammy, there's somebody at the door. Mammy!'

There was a slight pause, and then the crying started again. There was the sound of a bolt being undone.

'Who is it?' a woman's voice asked through the half-opened door.

'It's Tony,' said Tucker. 'Tony Tucker, and a pal of mine.'

The woman opening the door had a thin sweatshirt and jeans, and she was carrying a small boy of about three with a dummy tit in his mouth, placed there to stop him crying. He was sucking on it furiously. It made a smacking noise. She had a pale complexion, and tired eyes, concentric black rings ground into puckered skin. She gave a half-smile at Tucker, and then just looked at me warily.

'How's it going, Sandra?' asked Tucker cheerily. 'We were

just up the hill, so we thought we'd pop in for a wee cup of tea.'

There was a scratching at the door from the outside. The child's sucking stopped momentarily. He looked terrified.

'That's his dog,' said Tucker. He emphasized the 'his'. 'It's been chasing rabbits through all the shite of the day, so we thought we'd better leave it outside. It's all right.'

'Wee Kyle here loves dogs', she said, her eyes starting to smile. The baby sucked again. Then the smile fled. 'It hasn't got a rabbit with it, has it?' she asked. Her fear seemed to be conducted through her body to her child, whose eyes folded into fear. But there was no noise from him.

I told her that Keeper never caught any rabbits. He just liked to chase them.

She went to make some tea. She carried the cups in one at a time, as if she couldn't trust herself with a tray or a cup in each hand, and then went back for a jam sandwich for the boy. Tucker sat back in his seat and asked her to tell me what happened that night up in the shop. He didn't have to be any more specific than that. She had been called on to tell that story a hundred times. It was like asking somebody to give their testimony – the Road to Damascus experience, except here there was no blinding light, here there was no salvation.

'I'm still bad with my nerves you know,' she said. Her facial expression was flat, as if worn out with emotion. But it was probably just the effects of the tablets that her doctor would no doubt be prescribing. She held her son tightly.

'It was a Monday in February the night they came. It was a very windy night, dead blowy. I remember the door of the shop kept blowing open. It was the wee video shop where I worked.

'Do you know it?' she asked me.

117

I said that I had often passed it, but that I had never been in.

'He works hard at school this lad,' said Tucker. 'He's a bit of a smart baaaalicks.'

'Oh,' she said. 'A bit educated then?'

Neither of us mentioned the fact that I had walked out during an exam and never went back.

The child was beginning to watch us. He had turned round, and was starting to sit up. He was holding his jam sandwich.

'I was supposed to be working with my husband, Martin, that night, but it was his lodge night. Martin's sister owns the shop, and I had only been working there part-time for just two weeks. Just to get a wee bit of money.

'My husband's in the Orange Order, so he asked this young lad David to cover for him. It was my first night working with David since I started the job. It was meant to be Martin there that night. It was meant to be him. I don't mean that it was him they were after, I just mean that it was meant to be him working that particular night.'

She sat for a moment, letting the full significance of this sink in. Her eyes moved away from me, and drifted off. She did not like what she saw down there. She started again. 'It could have been my husband there that night.'

Her three-year-old son started to climb all over her. He started eating the sandwich. He was watching us more now. I noticed that the boy had scratches all around his eyes. Sandra's eyes looked sore as well from crying.

'You see we had it all arranged for me and Martin to work nights. The neighbour next door, who's a friend of ours, had offered to baby-sit at nights. We had to get the two boys and the wee girl in bed. They'd run around for an hour, then they'd go to bed. We could have worked that night, but Martin swapped shifts with David. I had come on at six, David had come on at five. Martin was there until about

118

seven, then he went off for his tea. It was about ten to eight, and I had just put three under the sunbeds upstairs. When I came down, David had made the coffee for the pair of us. I was putting a tape on. We were going to watch a wee film. It was *Out For Justice*. Martin always laughs about that film, people get hit in it with automatic fire, and when they're falling over they still manage to fire off their own guns. But living here we know that's all a bit far-fetched.'

Tucker was nodding his head and smiling. 'It's all just made up in the films. It's not realistic.'

I felt myself smiling as well, not because I was happy, just because I wanted to cheer her up. I wanted to tell the story of my friend pouring Ribena down a crack in the pavement to prove that a young Catholic had been bumped off up our way. I'd never seen anything like that in a film. I thought she might find the story funny, then I changed my mind as I looked at those eyes, rubbed raw and sore.

'I had just bent down and got the tape into the machine,' she said. 'Suddenly, this guy just flung the door of the shop wide open. He was standing there with a black-and-white check mask covering his face. It was like a sweatshirt that had been cut up with just a hole for his eyes. He didn't say anything. He didn't ask for anybody. He had the gun inside his coat. He pulled it out. I turned round to grab David but the gun started going off.'

Tucker was transfixed or acting transfixed. He had heard the story before. But she needed a captive audience, to tell her that this was all true and that she had come through it, that this was not some hideous nightmare, just something in her mind, that had destroyed her life. This was life and she had managed to live through it.

'David just sat there,' she said. 'By the time I grabbed him, he had already been hit. He fell across my legs on the floor behind the sweetie counter. There was bullets flying all around me.'

119

Her eyes were dead. She was talking about live bullets flying all over the place and her eyes were still dead. She lit another cigarette.

'Imagine sitting down on your settee one afternoon with a wee cup of tea in your hand and making a mask out of a sweatshirt, knowing what you're going to use it for,' said Tucker. 'You'd have to be a right fucking bastard – excuse my language – to do something like that. It's so . . .'

'Callous,' I suggested.

'Not human,' said Tucker.

Sandra sat there, with no emotion, deadened. She waited until we finished our little exchange, our irrelevant tittle-tattle about planning and motivation and preparation for the run into the shop as the masked man, the Lone Ranger, the SAS man abseiling down the walls of the Iranian Embassy, Batman, the man with the mask made out of a sweatshirt. Then she resumed her tale about the arbitrariness of life, and the way that fate flips you malevolently from something we know to something we can never know. My mind flitted to wet Mondays in the mission hall, and what I heard and read for two lollies, and to the clay of Roselawn where the earth is sucked out by spades in neat square shapes because the clay is so wet. Not so much buried as drowning in the wet earth. I knew that one day I was going to drown in that clay. Sometimes I felt like I was drowning already.

'David was an innocent wee lad,' she said. 'He would have thought that he was going to be robbed. That's how innocent he was. It would never have crossed his mind that he was going to be murdered.'

There were tears now. Silent tears crawling down her face, hanging at the end of her chin. One dripped on to the child. They left streaks. I knew they would. Salty tears always leave traces on your face.

'That's the kind of boy he was,' she said. 'He wouldn't have dreamt that somebody had come into the shop to take his life. He would have thought he was going to be robbed right until the last moment.'

Tucker looked at me as if to say, Have you heard enough? Do you see what we're dealing with in this city? But Sandra was locked into her tale, reliving it. She failed to notice that Tucker was signalling that she had said enough, that she had done her job. I needed to say something to help her.

'You would think that you were going to get robbed,' I said. 'If you were working in a shop that's what you would assume was happening. It's only natural.'

It was as if I had not spoken. Her flat worn face said nothing in the silence between her turns. For a second I thought she might not have heard me, that trauma might affect what you can hear, what you can take in. So I tried again.

'If you're in a shop, even in Belfast, and some big guy comes in with a gun, you'd just assume that they were after your money. You'd never think that they were going to shoot you dead. It wouldn't cross your mind. Until it was too late.'

Tucker nudged me to shut up. Only then did she wipe her face and resume her story and you could see the dampened-down twitches and grimaces increase as the gun was pulled out of a coat, and the bullets flew.

'Yer man just pulled the gun out and opened up. He just opened up. David was hit in the chest and the side. He was hit ten times. The gunman just ran out. I couldn't move.'

Her actions now mirrored the story. Her hands froze in the middle of a gesture. She had iconically re-enacted the shooting of an automatic weapon, and the clenched fists grasping the weapon had opened to show how he had run out. These splayed fingers now stopped. Her expression stopped along with it, and you could read the panic in her face, the blind terror, just as if somebody had pressed pause on the video to enjoy a piece of manufactured horror. But this was for real. It was not enjoyable to watch.

Tucker looked away, and shifted uncomfortably in his seat. He was counting faces in her coal fire. It was something that he always did when he was embarrassed. I joined him. I saw the faces at the back of the fire grinning. No teeth, wide gummy smiles. Red slits for mouths.

'I just sat there behind the counter,' she said. She looked at me, and I could feel myself respond. I was desperate to help her in her grief.

'Yeah?' I said.

'I didn't move until the fella next door came in. He had heard all the shooting. I didn't see a getaway car or anything. It just happened all that quick. I couldn't understand why I didn't get hit myself. I was as close to David as my child is now – that's the way the two of us were, shoulder to shoulder. David said something when he was shot, but I couldn't make it out. David was lying there on the ground, he was still alive. He was moving a bit, his arm and that, and his head. Then this nurse, who was visiting a relative up our way, came in. She tried to resuscitate David, but there was nothing she could do. I was just sitting there in a state of shock. I was crying. I didn't really know what was going on.'

Her son started crying again. She picked him up. His face was smeared with jam. 'My wee boy has been very hard to settle since we came up to this new estate. We're new up here. They've been bullying him at school, because he's new. They've scratched the eyes off him today, and cut his arm. They've trailed the eyes off him. But we had to move up here.'

She motioned towards the window. 'We're safe up here.'

'You're not safe anywhere in this town,' said Tucker. I knew it wasn't what he meant to say. But it didn't matter. She didn't really hear him. Tucker wanted to help, so he took me out to get some coal for her. She followed us out with her child, as if she couldn't bear to be on her own. The dark nights were coming in, and it was getting cold. Her child was shivering in her arms, but I don't think she felt the cold, or really noticed that her child was cold. She wanted company, and she wanted to talk.

Tucker opened the coal bunker and dug the shovel into the sharp black heap. 'The Friday after the shooting in the shop,' she said, 'I was standing in my hall in my house in Mountbatten Street, and I heard this other shooting.'

She needed to talk about her experiences. I don't think that Tucker wanted to listen any more. She had done her job. He could tell by my face that I had heard enough. She held her son tightly in her arms. 'I'd just come home from work,' she said. 'I'd just come through the door when I heard the bang.'

Tucker was just going, 'Yeah' quietly, not encouraging her, quite the opposite in fact. It was as if he wanted her to finish so that I would keep the story about David fresh in my mind. He didn't want me to be distracted by other stories, other experiences which had ripped her apart.

But she didn't respond. 'I just ran into the sitting room,' she said, 'and grabbed my youngest and ran straight upstairs. I had to get away from there. Unity Flats was just across from us. I didn't feel safe there. We were also petrol-bombed in our previous house in Cyprus Street one eleventh night. We were having a wee drink, and enjoying the bonfires, and suddenly these petrol bombs came flying in. I never felt safe down there.'

We stood in that cold dark yard listening to her. I could hear a helicopter in the night sky. Tucker and I looked up to see a distant single light. She didn't bother looking. She probably didn't hear it. The child looked into the sky to see what we were looking at, then he looked back at us, expectantly. I smiled at him. He didn't smile back, he just kept sucking and sucking on that dummy tit in his mouth and staring at us, watching us.

'At least up here is more secure than either of those other

123

two places,' she said. 'If they wanted to get you in here, they'd have to drive right up into the estate through some Protestant areas. They'd never make it up here and get back out. It's full of culs-de-sac. Or they'd have to come across the back fields from where the car they used in the murder was dumped, and get back over there again. An army helicopter would spot them on their way back, there's an army base near here. Surely they'd be spotted.'

You could tell that she was trying to reassure herself, as much as persuade us. Tucker was telling her that there was no way that the helicopter wouldn't spot them. In the end, Tucker had to suggest going back inside. He carried the coal in for her, and we all trooped back into the house in a long solemn line. We all sat back down on exactly the same seats again.

'I feel safe up on the estate, but it's very isolated,' she said. 'It's like a desert island. There's only the one shop. You have to get a black taxi down the road, and sometimes you're waiting for an hour and a half. There are buses, but we can only afford the black taxis.'

I looked out of Sandra's house across the fields to where her attackers had come from. 'It's about a mile to where they came from,' she said. I thought it was closer to two or three hundred yards. I sat there thinking that the mind can do wonderful things when it has to.

'You see what's so upsetting was that David was just a wee Christian boy,' she said. 'He was an innocent wee lad, God love him. They were in that shop for anybody that night. I read in the papers that the IPLO claimed it. They issued a statement a week later that they had carried out the shooting, because the shop was a front for the Organization. That was bloody nonsense. Somebody had seen a particular car parked outside the shop, a bit like the car of this guy who's meant to be in the Organization. Anyway, they'd seen the car and they'd put two and two together and made six. It might have been the same make of car, but it wasn't the same car. Don't they check registration numbers? Don't they check anything?'

'They check fuck all, and that's the truth,' said Tucker. 'Any excuse and they get the gun out. They don't even need an excuse.'

I was looking for signs that she was taking some of this in, but there was none. There was no connection. She was on her own, and she knew it, living with what had happened, trying to tell us. But we hadn't been there, and the things that we had seen over the years did not qualify us to understand this. She gripped her young son even more tightly. Perhaps he understood more, he had to live with her.

'This operation was meant to be based on IPLO intelligence work,' she said. 'I've never met a more innocent wee boy than David. He had just left school. He was only working in the shop part-time. He had got an interview coming up with C&A. You would always see him with people, never sure whether to say hello or not. A shy wee boy. Then some bad pig comes in and does that. He had his whole life in front of him. This operation was meant to be based on intelligence. But what kind of intelligence turns a wee seventeen-year-old into a legitimate target?'

Sandra smoothed her son's hair. 'I've found it hard to get over the murder. I'm going to the doctor every other week. He's got me on tablets for my nerves. I can't sleep at night. I keep having flashbacks. I was scared when I heard that the IPLO done it. I was always scared of them coming back and recognizing me. I was scared of them coming after me. I think the IPLO are younger than the IRA and more ruthless. The IRA hit the security forces, the IPLO don't seem so particular. I tried to go back to work, but it wasn't good for my nerves. Every time the door blew open, I would jump. I realized I wasn't going to be able to do it any more. My husband still works there. He says that you have to go on.

You can't give in to intimidation. If you did, then the IPLO or the IRA would just hit one shop after another, until all the Protestant shops were closed. My husband still brings our six-year-old daughter to the shop with him. But only in the afternoons after school, I wouldn't let him bring her at nights. I'd be too worried.'

Her son was crying again. His elbow was sore, it had started bleeding. She stroked his forehead, trying to calm him down. She laid him down on the settee, stroking him, calming him. She was also trying to calm herself. Her youngest was waking up in the next room. He was nearly two. She carried him in, he was sucking a dummy tit too. He was fiddling with the ends of her hair, and trying to get back to sleep.

'We called him Patrick,' she said, 'because we thought we could do our bit for reconciliation on this island. I've got a cousin called Patrick in Canada. It's a lovely name. You don't have to be a Taig to be called Patrick. There's a lot of Protestants in Canada called Patrick.'

She stroked Patrick's short stocky legs. He started to wake up, blinking. He looked at Tucker and me.

'Patrick knew David. David was great with kids. He would come round here and play with the wee child. Wait until you hear this. Patrick, where's David? Where's David?'

The child had large brown eyes which opened wide. His hands lifted upwards and turned palms up.

'Gone,' he said.

'Where's David?'

'Gone.'

'Where's David?'

'All gone.'

I left her in that house on the desert island and Tucker and I made our way over the walls of the culs-de-sac to the road and then through another estate to the video shop where the shooting had occurred. He said that there was somebody else I should meet, that the shooting that cold

February night was not the first time that the IPLO had decided the shop was a legitimate target. Five months before the murder, there was an attempt on the life of the woman who owned the video shop, on the road outside, as she and her brother were closing up for the night. Tucker took me to the video shop to talk to Martin, Sandra's husband, who had witnessed the whole thing. Martin looked pleased to see Tucker, happy to have some company. He was tall, and he bent over towards you when he talked. He sat behind the sweetie counter: 'We'd only put this in the day David was hit.'

Tucker asked Martin to tell me about the attempt on his sister's life. Martin didn't hesitate. He too looked as if this was a natural request. He said, 'Hang on a minute,' and he lit up a cigarette. He wanted to get himself ready for the story. 'I saw the car pull up in front of her,' he said. 'I thought it was this taxi driver that she'd just waved at. I got into my van, and I watched the car pull up. I thought to myself, I'll wait and see what's happening here. The next minute I saw yer man run out with the gun. He had a hood on. He ran out right in front of her. Here's me, What the hell? I tried to do something in the van. I was beeping the horn, flashing the lights – trying to draw attention to what was going on. When I looked at yer man I saw that he had the gun and he was hitting it. It must have jammed or something because he couldn't get it cocked. He tried to shoot her three times but it just wouldn't fire. He never budged – he just stood still staring straight at Jackie's car.'

Martin had the cigarette jammed in his mouth. The smoke drifted up into his eyes. Martin was acting the assassin, staring straight at the car. The smoke was making him blink.

'I was beeping away,' he said, 'but it didn't put him off. There were loads of cars flying past, but they didn't stop. Jackie had just frozen. She couldn't get her car in gear. She told me she was just sitting there wondering which part of her body the bullets would strike and how much it was going to hurt. But yer man's gun just wouldn't fire, so he jumped back into his car, and he and this other guy drove off. It was like something out of a film. It was unbelievable. I eventually got my own car into gear and gave him a bit of a chase around the Gleneagle Road, then I thought I'd better get back and see how my sister was. She was a bit shaken, I'll tell you that. You don't get over that sort of thing for a while. The ones who killed David used exactly the same escape route. Everybody knew it was the same gunman in both. It was the same MO in both cases.

'But it didn't put me off working in the shop. My attitude is that somebody could walk in here at any time, pull out a gun and then you're gone. You've had it. I'd just be with my ma, who died last year.'

The door was banging. Martin sat there calmly, looking out on to the grey street. Customers filed in and out of the shop.

'As Jackie says, there are about seventeen hundred customers who come here. A security door would do you no good. You wouldn't be able to recognize them all. Any gunman would still be able to slip in. There's not a lot you can do, and we all know it.'

We watched the customers in the shop, some with their backs to us. Every one a potential killer. Some spending too long looking at a particular title. Any moment, I thought, any moment. This was what Tucker wanted.

'The shooting put people off for a couple of weeks, it's bound to,' said Martin. 'But after about three weeks they started coming back. We opened up the shop again the Friday after David was murdered. Plenty of people came in to say they were pleased to see that we'd opened up so quickly, but a couple of the locals said that we opened again too soon. But you can't give in to terror. If you do, you're beat.'

Tucker put his hand on Martin's shoulder. I had never seen him display affection quite so openly before. He patted Martin's shoulder lightly.

'I've told my wife, If they do get me, then you just carry on without me,' said Martin. 'I haven't missed a day here since the shooting. You can't let them put you off. We have to try and live as normal a life as possible.'

'That's good,' said Tucker. 'You can't give in to them. No way. I bet you can't even have a day off on the sick when this kind of thing happens, in case people think you're running scared.'

'Exactly,' said Martin. 'You can't even be sick any more. After they tried to kill Jackie, we all discussed the situation between ourselves in the shop. We put it down to the fact that Jackie had just got a new car that very week which was very similar to this local guy in the Organization. We thought that it was an attempt on his life, that it was nothing to do with Jackie as such – even though the gunman that night knew it was a woman in the car in front of him. If his gun hadn't jammed, he would have killed her. I said to David when he started work, "What would happen if me and you were sitting here, and a gunman comes through the door?" And he says to me, "What could you do? There's not much you could do in a situation like that. You'd be shot dead and that's about it."'

Tucker looked at me, and nodded. 'There's not much you can do when that happens to you,' he said to Martin. 'Your number's up basically, and when your number's up, your number's up. It's between you and the big fella upstairs after that.'

'Too fucking right,' said Martin. He took a long deep draw on his cigarette. He looked as if he needed his wee smoke. 'Too fucking right,' he said again.

'The funny thing is that it hasn't made me think about moving from the area,' said Martin. 'I've got a sister over in

England and she says to me, "Why don't you and your family move over here with me?" She can't understand why we don't want to move. But it would be a different country over there across the water. It would be like being born again. You'd have to start a new life. I don't know anything about life over there. One of our neighbours moved to England, but she only stuck it for a couple of months. You get used to the people that you're living with. Belfast is the only place I've ever known. It's my wee home, and you shouldn't be driven from your home, no matter what they do.'

I had started to tear at a bus ticket that I had been fiddling with all that afternoon. The ticket was in shreds. I watched Martin's eyes reflect on what could easily be. The wind was getting worse, and even I commented on what a blowy night it had become. Every time the door blew open I jumped inside.

'Have you heard my wee boy Patrick talking about his uncle David?' asked Martin. 'That's what we call him, "Uncle David", even though he wasn't really his uncle. But it's amazing that my wee boy even remembers him. My wee boy was only one year old when David was killed after all. But the wife always shows the wee one David's photograph to remind him.'

Martin took another long draw on his cigarette, hollowing his cheeks. He looked gaunt and tired. 'It breaks my heart when he says, "Gone" when she takes the photograph away,' said Martin. 'It breaks my fucking heart.'

Tucker put his hand on Martin's shoulder again, and squeezed. We just silently nodded and left the shop. Tucker didn't speak, which was rare for him. We walked up the entry in silence. You could hear the *click-clack* of the metal guard on Tucker's shoes on the pavement. Somewhere in the night sky we could hear the helicopter still humming in the distance. It was shining its light on some fields between Sandra's house and the grey distant republican streets where some men plan terrible actions, callous actions. Not even human action, according to Tucker. I noticed that on the wall at the back of the sweetie shop some new concrete had been laid with bits of jagged glass sticking out of it. It would still be easy to get over it, I thought to myself; they had forgotten to close up the foothold half-way up the wall. You would have to be careful though.

'It's not the money, you know,' Tucker said quietly without looking at me. 'That was just a bonus the other day. Just a bonus.'

We walked on, the streets quiet apart from the humming in the sky, a light somewhere in the distance. He stopped suddenly, and turned to me.

'I know you're still a bit unsure about all of this. Aren't you?'

'A bit,' I said, 'because I don't know where any of it leads. You don't want to end up like Kingo's da, do you?'

'I don't want to end up like David either,' said Tucker, 'falling down dead over a sweetie counter, and nobody able to make out my last words. You've got to fight fire with fire. I don't agree with everything Kingo's da stands for, but he makes some sense.

'Anyway, you just think of that wee child every time you have second thoughts. Just think of the wee child saying "Gone." That's what I do. Just think of him saying fucking gone, and then tell me that you think that we should sit on our fucking arses and do nothing.'

9

It was Saturday night. Tucker said he would get me into the club. He said that now there was no stopping us.

The club. That's all they called it up our way. 'Are you going to the club?' they'd say. It was the place to be, and it had been for years ever since O'Shea's had been burnt down, fire-bombed by the locals one Saturday night when they'd been drinking, because they didn't like a Taig operating in our community like that.

Even though he had been there for years and knew them all by name. Even though he knew what all of them drank, and what they owed behind the bar. That's right, he gave them all credit. He knew they'd pay him back because deep inside he knew that they were all basically honourable people. And besides he knew that they had nowhere else to go.

That night he watched his bar burn from up the hill, and he never came back down. Not even in the middle of the day with the men from the insurance company, with all the RUC men milling about. He left that to his sons. He drove past the burnt-out shell a few times, but he never looked, he never wanted to see the place where he had spent so much of his life building up business and good will. Good will, that's a joke, he thought, whenever he saw heaps of charred beams and ashes anywhere in that town.

Then the Organization opened the club down behind where O'Shea's had once stood. The club constructed out of pebbledashed concrete block, the club down the entry behind a cage. Security was tight, with metal bars covering every window. And you had to be in the know to get in.

Tucker was in the know now and I was his mate. It was as simple as that. I told my mother where I was going. She told me to look out to see if Ernie still drank there. That was his haunt, so he told the girls at work. But she wasn't sure.

The cameras watched us walk up to the heavy metal door, with rivets down the outside, and a large rusty dent towards the bottom.

'Ram raiders,' said Tucker, noticing the dent. 'It must have been ram raiders – desperate for a drink.'

You could hear the security cameras creak as they followed us around. There was a wire grille over the top of the door-way to stop anybody trying to lob a bomb over with an under-arm motion. The metal door creaked open. Tucker stood there in the harsh glare of the security light with his hands on his hips.

'Yes?' said a grey-haired man with a cigarette in his hand peeking out from behind the door. He half sat on a red threadbare stool and swivelled his long scrawny neck so that he could see us. We could see him sitting in front of a bank of video monitors, with slow-moving images of barbed wire and wire grille and small contracted men with caps and bald heads, the club scanned from every angle. The IRA would have loved to have got that club, even on a Wednesday night which was pensioner night when the old folks as my mother called them, or the coffin dodgers as we called them, were invited in to play bingo. A full house. Fathers and mothers and uncles and aunts of known hard-line loyalists sitting down to play. Not just any coffin dodgers, these. There would be some tears in hard-line families in the loyalist community if they managed to smuggle a gun past that door when all eyes were down on the cards in front of them. All the sixes, clickety-click. And a lot of tears in more ordinary households as well.

The man with his arse half on the stool had watched us walk up to the door and obviously thought that, although we were strangers, we weren't dangerous strangers, as he put his head round the door and straight in our view.

'What do you want?' he said.

'We want a drink,' said Tucker.

There was a slight pause.

'That's what we want.'

There was another pause, longer this time, achingly long. We were new to this game. We didn't quite know how to act like big shots. Not yet anyway.

'We're here for a drink, if that's all right with you,' said Tucker again. The tone was sarcastic. Too sarcastic, I thought, for men down an entry in the glare of a security light.

'It's a private club,' said the grey-haired man. 'Fuck away off. You're only young lads. Just fuck off home to your mothers.'

'We're members,' said Tucker. Then, after a pause, 'New members.'

'I don't know you,' said the man peeking out from behind the door. 'And if I don't know you then you're not members. There's no fucking way that I know you, so you're not members. So fuck away off.'

I noticed that there was a logic to all of this. Not much compassion or understanding, but logic. It was a job that clearly required logic.

'We're friends of Mr King,' said Tucker.

There was another pause. This time a thinking pause. A pause filled with silence but not a vacuum.

'Which Mr King?' said the security man. 'Mr Thomas King? Mr Philip fucking King? Or Mr fucking Colin fucking King?'

'Mr Philip King,' said Tucker.

The door slammed shut. But we could hear the security

man leaving his post, walking across the hard concrete floor behind the bomb-proof front door.

Tucker stood there whistling, his hands in his pockets, looking up at the camera, smiling, winking.

'Some security this,' said Tucker. 'You could blow this door and there would be nobody there to raise the alarm.'

A moment later, the door swung open. Kingo's da stood there smiling.

'Come on in lads. Sorry about that. This is Besty, our security specialist. He had to give you the once-over.'

Besty nodded across to us in a cursory and unfriendly way, and kept his eyes fixed on the column of video screens, as if logic dictated that the moment after the door has been opened is the most dangerous of all.

'We're on amber alert tonight,' said Kingo's da. 'Somebody rang up with a bomb warning, but Besty just thinks it was somebody who he barred from the club for falling asleep in the toilet. He thinks that, but he doesn't know it. So that's why we're only on amber. But still you have to be on your toes.'

Besty did not look happy as we brushed past him and into the smoky atmosphere of the club. I noticed that every table was taken. I could see the eyes follow us, sly eyes practised at watching. We stood out. New members. Or rather a new member and his mate. I followed Tucker and Kingo's da through the club, between the tables. Hands would gently touch Kingo's da on the way through. Gentle squeezes, as if he had been away for a long time, and not just to the security door and back. Kingo's da took us to his table. A long crescent-shaped seat in red crushed velour with himself in the middle, facing the entrance. Two men of a similar age on either side of him, one with a moustache and one with a shaved head and very broad shoulders. And two blonde heavily made-up women on the outer edges of the crescent. Tucker noticed these immediately.

135

'Rides', would have been Tucker's normal description. 'Big fucking rides'. But Tucker would be watching his talk tonight.

Kingo's da made a space for us beside him. The women inched their heavy bottoms to the very edges of the crescent. I noticed that one wore French knickers under tight brown polyester trousers. You could see the outline of the frills as she cocked her arse to edge across the seat. The drinks arrived, without us having to ask. Two pints of lager. They looked a bit flat, as if they had been standing for a while, but you couldn't have said anything. Every now and then some man passing came up to our table and whispered something to Kingo's da. They were probably asking what he was drinking, because every now and then more drink would mysteriously arrive. They might, however, have been discussing other things. Tucker was brought into the conversation, and I just sat there watching the faces of the men at the tables around us. Men with sad watery eyes, the drink doing their talking for them.

That's what my mother always said. It's the drink talking. 'There are some big men in those loyalist clubs and no doubt in republican clubs, until the morning,' she liked to say.

I watched Tucker and Kingo's da have a good laugh. Two more pints arrived. This time they weren't flat. The hum of conversation was getting louder, louder and more diffuse. Words were coming from other tables. It was hard to make sense of the conversations even if you really tried, half whispered, conspiratorial at times, the sounds rising and falling. Some words clear and audible, others not. Whole sentences were disappearing into the void of whispers and silences behind the palm of the hand. 'Whatever you say, say nothing' was one of Kingo's da's favourite expressions. Nudges and winks, and occasionally the face would set hard and violent. I heard one whole sentence from this particular face on the table next to us: 'His fucking number's up,' then the voice dipped again, and I was lost. I watched Tucker again and he was enjoying himself. He was getting all the attention. He winked at me, but the hum just continued.

There was a photograph of the Queen on the wall. It was a very old photograph with a slightly green tinge to it. She was young, half smiling. Her lips had gone black. I could just about see the smile through the haze of smoke. I felt quite alone and was now leaving the decoding of the hum to others, until I heard Tucker mention the idea for the cleaning service, his brainwave for informing clients about the date and times of collections. The word 'Glenview' seized my attention.

I heard Kingo's da erupt with laughter. They were all laughing, even Tucker, who had managed somehow in his account to transfer this ludicrous idea from himself to me. The hum of conversation stopped momentarily. There was just the heavy chesty sound of laughter, with Kingo's da and the man with the moustache, and the man with the broad shoulders, and the blonde women and Tucker all looking at me.

'Different, fucking different,' said Kingo's da, pretending that he was hearing the idea for the first time. 'I think we may put that idea on hold for the moment.' His laughter was being exhaled through a half-open mouth, it was wheezing out through his chest and mouth.

Kingo's da was patting Tucker's shoulder. 'But it's good that you can twist the arms of your mates to give a bit of thought into ways of improving our operations. It's good that you've been thinking about us.'

Kingo's da looked at me almost pityingly. The woman to my right leant forward to talk to me. I could see down her yellow silky top. 'I think that Glenview Cleaning Services is a lovely idea,' she said. Her speech was slurred. Tucker pressed the side of his hard bony knee against the side of my leg, just in case I hadn't noticed what was down her top.

He kept it pressed there to emphasize that I should take a long look. He was making a gentle sucking noise, inhaling air through his teeth, but much quieter than usual. Kingo's da would probably have thought it was Tucker's asthma.

A man came over to our table. He had a fat red face. It was the face of a man with dangerously high blood pressure. His shirt was too tight, the fat on his neck bulged out around it, a thick wad hanging over his collar. The collar was soiled, his arteries constrained. He was ostensibly talking to Kingo's da, but he was really talking to us all. He was probably in his early forties, but that took a lot of working out from the dates he had been throwing around. His face said late fifties. He had seen it all, and that red puffy face told you so. He'd had a bad week.

'Yer man just waved me down. I thought he was a fare. Then he pulled the mask up, like the Lone Ranger. He just said, "Get out of the fucking car." The window was up, so I tried to bluff him. I thought to myself, Just pretend you're daft. I was saying to him, "Sorry I can't hear ye." So yer man says, "Wind the fuckin' window down." He's making all these winding movements. So I thinks to myself, I'd better pretend that I'm a bit fucking stupid. He might feel sorry for me that way. But I thought to myself, I'd better get the window down all the same, otherwise he'll put it through. Your man's playing with his waistband – something's stuck down there. Eventually he gets it out. It's a big fuckin' gun. I'm no expert on guns, Philip. You know that.'

Kingo's da nodded to us all.

'That's true enough, Tommy.'

The man with the moustache laughed.

'I've had one or two pushed in my kisser before,' said Tommy. 'But that's about it. I don't touch them, I never have. I want nothing to do with them. Isn't that right, Philip?'

The man with the moustache nodded.

'Anyway,' said Tommy. 'I'm just staring at the muzzle and

thinking to myself, Holy fuck. So your man starts pointing it at me. He's saying, "Get out of the car you big fat fucker." I thought I was hearing things. I couldn't believe it. He wasn't satisfied with just doing a hijacking, he was starting to insult me as well. He was a skinny wee shite as well. So I got out of my taxi, and he says, "Get up against the wall you big fat cunt." So I tried to appeal to him. I tried appealing to his better nature. I said, "Look mate, you've got me up against the wall. Don't take my car. It's all I've got. If you take my car, I'll be on the brew, I'll be a statistic." So at that point, he starts to get very agitated. He says to me, "I'll make you a statistic all right. I'll fuckin' well shoot you, you big fat bastard." So I'm standing there. It's pelting with rain, and I'm pleading with this wee shite not to take my car. He's the fella in the big picture because he's got this gun. They call them joyriders. Joyriders my arse. He was a fuckin' hijacker. I'd no idea what he wanted my car for. They found it burnt out later. I don't know what it had been used for, and quite frankly I don't care.'

Kingo's da was shaking his head. 'Where was this exactly?'

'Stonepark,' said Tommy.

'Fucking Stonepark,' said Kingo's da. 'I thought so, dangerous ground. Dangerous fucking ground. Lawless. No man's land.'

The man with the moustache repeated, 'No man's land.' He was not only echoing Kingo's da's words, he was echoing his facial movements. Kingo's da looked disgusted, so did the man with the moustache. They both released that look at exactly the same time. It was odd to watch.

'My son had to loan me the money to buy my new car,' said Tommy. 'He had to take out a loan on it, and then lend it to me. I've only had this new car two days. I swear to God that if any wee shite with a scarf over his face jumps in front of this car, I'll run him over, so help me God. You're always on your guard around here. They think they're the fella in the big picture all right. You could beat most of them with your cap, if they weren't carrying.'

'Exactly,' said Kingo's da. 'Exactly. That's what we're up against in this town – lawlessness. No respect for the rule of law. They've got a gun and they think they can dictate to the rest of us.'

Tommy was sweating. 'But when they pull out a gun,' he said, 'what can you do? When they get the gun out, then they know that you're going to comply with whatever they say. They can do what they want, and they know it.'

Kingo's da took a long thoughtful drink from his lager.

'The truth is', said Tommy, 'that I don't know whether he was one of ours or one of theirs. Sometimes there's nothing to separate them. Each side is as bad as the other.'

'I wouldn't go that far,' said Kingo's da. 'But fair point. There's a lot of Billy the Kids on both sides.'

'Wild men,' said the man with the moustache.

'Boys with little dicks trying to make themselves look bigger,' said the big blonde beside Tucker.

'But he was a nervous little shite,' said Tommy. 'He's probably had an accident by now pulling that gun out of his waistband. So if you see somebody walking around Belfast with half a dick, just ask him why he hijacked my car.'

'If he didn't have just half a dick before,' said the blonde again.

'Don't lower the tone for fuck's sake,' said Kingo's da. 'We've got company here with us tonight.'

Tommy touched Kingo's da's hand. 'I'm getting off, Philip. If you hear what happened to my car or find out who took it, I'm sure that you'll have a word in their ear for me.'

'You can count on it,' said Kingo's da. 'If he's one of ours I'll get to know, don't worry about that. I'll ask around. If he's one of ours I'll have a word with him for you.'

Tommy thanked him and wove his way back across the club to his two friends.

Kingo's da turned to Tucker. 'This town's in danger of becoming like something out of the Wild West, if we don't do something about it. The RUC don't want to know, as long as we're shooting each other they're quite content to let us get on with it.'

From across the room, I could hear raised voices. A chair was knocked over. Kingo's da winked at the man with the moustache. He was across the room in no time. One elderly man was on his feet, swearing at a short, much younger man. The old man was gripping a brown parcel, something that he had smuggled into the club. There was a tussle between the elderly man and the man from our table, and the brown parcel he was holding fell to the ground and spilt open. I could see a half dozen pigs' feet sliding out of the paper, and inching their way across the dirty floor. The man with the moustache let go of the old man. The elderly man got down on his hands and knees and started to gather the pigs' feet up again. Nobody tried to help him. Then he sat down quietly.

The man with the moustache came back dusting his hands. 'It was old Bobby Hutcheson again,' he said. 'Johnny Hutch's da. I told him that we all knew it was difficult for him with his son inside, but one more time and we'd have to bar him. It's as simple as that.'

'Quite right,' said Kingo's da. 'If he wants to stay as a member here, he has to obey the rules like anybody else. Just because his son is serving our country behind bars doesn't grant him any special privileges in here. He has to learn to obey the rules.'

The man with the moustache took a long drink from his lager. 'I also told him that we were going to take his false teeth out and hold them captive until he starts to behave. That'll stop him winding everybody up.'

Kingo's da was snorting with laughter. The fat blonde with the French knickers said, 'Oh, that's awful.' But she was laughing as well.

'Was that pigs' feet your man had in his wee parcel by the way?' she asked. 'My wee dog loves pigs' feet. Could you ask him, Philip, if he doesn't want those pigs' feet now that they've been on the ground perhaps he'd give them to my wee Cindy. Cindy adores pigs' feet.'

I asked how old Cindy was. I told the fat blonde with the French knickers that I too was a dog lover.

'Really,' she said. 'Everybody loves dogs though, don't they? It's no wonder they do; they're better than humans. My wee Cindy would eat anything you put in front of her. She's not fussy. She even likes onions. I read that dogs don't like onions. But my wee dog adores onions. Does your dog like onions?'

I said that I wasn't sure. I didn't feed Keeper, so I wasn't sure what he liked. She assumed that I had just never tried giving him onions. She suggested I should try.

'The man who sold me Cindy told me never to give her onions,' she said, 'but that wasn't right. My wee Cindy loves onions. She just loves them. They're good for you as well, do you know that? They thin your blood. Did you know that?'

Before I got a chance to answer, the noise started again. The elderly man had a pig's foot in his hand and pushed it into the face of the other man. Kingo's da went this time. He took Mr Hutcheson by the arm and led him out of the club.

He was gone for a few minutes. He came back slightly out of breath. 'I had to give him a good talking-to', he said. 'He said he'd heard that somebody was seeing his daughter-in-law and accused wee Badger of it. He drinks with wee Badger nearly every night, that's the funny thing. That's what all the trouble was about. Wee Badger denied it, of course. I told

Johnny's da that he was paranoid, and that he had to get his act in order or he wouldn't be allowed back into the club. There's enough trouble in our wee town without starting it in your own back yard.'

The blonde with the French knickers was nodding away. 'You're just right, Philip. You have to have a word with these people, to show them who's boss. They wouldn't behave like this in their own houses, so why should they be allowed to do it here?' She looked around at us all for support. 'It was like that lad in here last week who was on the drugs. He didn't know where he was. I thought he was going to wreck the place.'

Kingo's da sat back. 'Let me just say one thing and we'll leave it at that, and we've got two young lads here tonight so it's very relevant. We can't tolerate drug-taking in our community. This young lad was on something, it was as clear as daylight. So he had to be asked to leave, and he was given a formal warning. We don't want any of that rubbish in our streets. If you two lads are offered anything, you come and see me and I'll sort the problem out. Don't worry about that. Now let's change the subject. Whose round is it for fuck's sake? It must be yours. You're the only one who hasn't bought a drink.'

Kingo's da looked straight at me. He was smiling. He knew that I had no money. As far as I could see nobody had bought a drink. They seemed to have all been on the house. I glanced at Tucker, but he couldn't help.

'You're not a tight wee bastard, are you?' said the man with the moustache.

Then I felt a large hand under the table touch my fingers and gently prise them apart. I could feel the sharp edges of a note being pushed into my hand. It was Kingo's da helping out, and doing it secretly.

'No, I'm no tight bastard,' I said and got up to go to the bar. I carried the drinks back on a tray with a picture of the

Houses of Parliament on it. The eyes in that bar had noticed who I was with, and it felt comfortable threading my way back. Strangers moved their chairs out of the way, and steadied their friends for me to pass. Tucker had moved to the outside of the crescent-shaped seat and was chatting to the blonde who wasn't wearing the French knickers. In fact, she didn't appear to be wearing any knickers. My mother used to say that there were good-time girls in Belfast who went out for a night out with their knickers in their handbag. But then again, she didn't really know about G-strings and things like that. She had never been to this sort of club, which attracted the more selective clientèle. More heavily selected than O'Shea's anyway. Tucker was trying to look down her top, but it was more difficult because it was tighter around the neck.

Kingo's da put his arm around the back of my seat, and leant closer. 'I liked your da, you know that, he was a good man.'

I made a low noise of agreement. Kingo's da's statement sounded like the typical bland platitude which people say when they have been drinking. A broad positive statement which is never followed up.

'I never knew he had a bad heart, until it all happened, you know,' he said.

It was a strange change in the direction of the conversation.

'I bet you don't remember him that well,' he said. 'It's funny that. The people who mean the most to you often fade the fastest. There's probably a good reason for that. I don't know what it is, but it stops you breaking your heart or something like that.'

He watched me closely, as if he was trying to read my face.

'I've got some pictures of him in the house. He was a lot older than me, of course, but I used to see quite a bit of him. I knew him very well. He used to talk about you and your schoolwork all the time when he was fixing my car. Or at the meetings.'

It was the vagueness in this last reference that got me going. It was a hook. I could see it in his eyes. Kingo's da was reeling me in.

'What meetings?' I asked.

'Don't be telling me your mother never told you. He used to come to our meetings. All the men who were in the defence associations, the vigilantes, used to go to the meetings. Your da was no different, you know. In fact, he was dedicated to saving Ulster. Me and him were a team, and a good team at that. The UDA sprang out of those meetings.'

I sat there, in the midst of all that noise, and I heard nothing. I had had my family history written for me, and it was a history of a family daring to stay out, daring to be different. A history of a gentleman in the family, who went out to the street to break wind, with men and women crying at the funeral. Now Kingo's da was telling me that there might be something that I knew nothing about. He didn't say it directly. He was too crafty for that. He implied it. He drew me in.

'Don't get me wrong,' he said. 'He was a good man but there are a lot of good men in the Organization fighting to save Ulster. We can't depend on anybody in the end. You know that, don't you? Not the politicians in Westminster, nor the Unionist politicians, nor big Ian. He's doing very well out of it all, thank you very much. There's nobody cares two damns about us. Nobody. Your da knew it, and I think you've started to realize it. You and Tucker both. Isn't that right?'

He squeezed my arm gently. But I didn't reply. So he squeezed it harder, until he got a noise out of me.

'Hum,' I said.

'You're one of us, whether you like it or not. That school confused you for a while. But now you're free of it, you can

145

be yourself. Your da would have been proud of you if you'd got involved. And you know that we have to stick together. On our own, we're nothing. We're fuck-all. We have to act together. We have to depend on each other.'

He glanced over at Tucker, who had now managed to find a better position for himself by edging up the back of the seat to feast on the mounds of white flesh in front of him.

'Take Tony over there. He's a good lad. Right? The two of you grew up together. Right? You can depend on each other. Right? Well it's just like that in the Organization. You're with your friends. Your mates. You can depend on each other. Your da knew all this, without anybody having to tell him. He used to sit in those old overalls of his at our meetings on his way home from work, and I knew he was one of us. Do you remember how those old overalls used to smell? Of course you do. They were stinking. He was a grafter, your da. You couldn't get rid of that smell. He'd come straight from work. That's how dedicated he was. And I think you'll turn out OK like him, now that you realize all that fucking Latin and maths isn't for the likes of you. Or me.

'Isn't that right?'

At a table somewhere in the smoke, a man had started singing. The song was 'Little Old Wine Drinker Me'. Kingo's da stared at me. 'Isn't that right?' he said again, as if he thought I might not have heard him. He nudged me with his elbow.

I wasn't sure what I was agreeing to, but I said yes anyway. I watched Tucker leave with the blonde woman with no knickers. He stood up and said that she had asked him to leave her home. Kingo's da nodded his agreement. I sat in silence in the unbearable hum of the club. Kingo's da was engaging others now. I was thinking about what he had said, I was desperate to hear more, but he was talking about other things now – Ulster's heritage, not just mine. I sipped the flat lager and then made some excuse and left. I couldn't see any sign of Tucker or his friend. I walked up the entry home, the blood pounding in my ears. There was a full moon lighting the entry, making dark, shadowy holes by the sides of the walls of the entry. Holes to fall into. I could see the jagged edges of the broken bottoms of bottles protruding from the tops of the walls, casting long dark pointed shadows. I climbed up the wall of somebody else's back yard, and on to the roof of a shed, and sat there.

None of what Kingo's da had said could possibly be true. Somebody would have told me all this before. My mother would have said *something*. There are some things that you must mention to make sense of a family. None of what Kingo's da had said made any real sense. But why did he say it then? I could feel big salty tears start to find the corners of my mouth. I sat there, hunched up against the cold and my own confused emotions, listening to distant cars, and cats screeching to be heard on the yard walls, wailing, demanding to be listened to.

Suddenly, I heard something right down below me, shuffling along by the side of the hedge. A noise like a large rat snouting the branches aside, snapping the twigs. I leant back over the wall and I could just make out a dark shadow on the ground by the back of the Elim. I could see a white face slide out of the hedge. It was Mr Hutcheson, his head bleeding. He was mouthing something. I could see that he had lost his false teeth.

'Help me, son,' he said through soft wet gaping gums. 'Help me to get home.'

I lifted him to his feet. He was still trying to keep hold of the pigs' feet in a burst brown bag. There were only three now in this bloody parcel. He told me that somebody had followed him out of the club and hit him from behind. He said he was sure it was Kingo's da. 'I saw his ring,' he said.

'I saw that fucking ring of his. The one that he's always showing off. The one with Arkle on it.'

He put his arm around my shoulder, and we inched our way towards his house.

'But why would he want to hurt an old man? Why would he want to lay a finger on an old man whose son is giving his life for the cause? Answer me that.'

I told him that I didn't know, that I had no answers, that I didn't know what was going through anybody's mind any longer. I helped him to his house and rang the doorbell. Before anybody answered, I hurried home. I saw a few lads at the corner. Billy was with them. I hadn't seen him for a while. But it wasn't that unusual for somebody to disappear for a while. They always came back, eventually. I waved at them. But I didn't feel like talking. Not even to my mates.

10

It was the beeping of the car that woke me up. The shrill, insistent tone with the gap in between – well, not much of a gap. Whoever it was was a bit impatient. I looked at the clock. It was just after eleven. My mother was still in bed.

'Somebody must have ordered a taxi,' she shouted in. 'I wish they'd get their lazy wee arse out of bed.'

I peered out through the net curtains of the top bedroom window, and saw Hammerhead hanging out of the passenger door of a bright red Celica, looking up at the window of my room. I pulled back the curtains and knocked the windowpane to attract his attention. He waved up. It was an excited sort of wave. I could see that his nose was still swollen.

'We've got some wheels. Hurry up,' he said. He didn't really say this, he was mouthing the words. Either he didn't want the neighbours to hear, or he thought that our walls were thicker than they looked, and that there was no point in actually shouting because I still wouldn't hear. He was good at mouthing words. Even back in primary school he was good at it. When the headmaster walked past, he would mouth 'Wanker,' but he did the hand action as well in those days. I could make out 'wheels' and 'Move it.' Or it might have been 'Get a move on.' On second thoughts it probably was that. He was probably saying 'Get a fucking move on.' Anyway, I knew what he meant. The wave told me everything that I wanted to know. That and the brand-new car sitting

149

in our street. The car that didn't belong to him. We were going for a day out, whether I liked it or not.

I jumped out of bed and pulled on my clothes. I didn't have time to wash my face. My mother had heard me knocking on the windowpane, and came into my room in her new dressing gown.

'What are you boys up to?' she said.

She knew already that we were up to something. I knew that because she had put her new dressing gown on. She would be coming down to the street with me to try to find out what was going on.

She had got the dressing gown for Christmas from Ernie, but she hadn't worn it before. She had kept it hanging from a nail on the back of her door for ten months. I thought she was trying to keep it good until next Christmas, so that she could wear it on Christmas Day and pretend that it was new, just in case she didn't get anything as good as this. She called it her housecoat.

'That's a lovely car, Thomas,' she said to Hammerhead.

'And that's a lovely dressing gown, Mrs Roberts,' said Hammerhead, who was an expert at evading the issue at times like this.

'I mean I haven't seen it before,' said my mother.

'It's my uncle's, Mrs Roberts,' said Hammerhead. 'He's just over from England for a wee holiday, so he is. He said I could borrow it, now that I've passed my test, and take the car for a wee spin down to Bangor.'

My mother went out into the street, pulling her housecoat tight around her.

'Look at me out on the street in my nightclothes,' she said even though she sometimes stayed in her housecoat, her old housecoat, that is, not the new one – all day at weekends when she had had enough of life in our street. She had a good look at the inside and the outside of the car, like someone about to purchase the vehicle. A thorough inspection, like the man from the AA. She was obviously looking for something, like loose wires as evidence of a car that had been hot-wired, but she couldn't find whatever she was looking for. Then she went back into the hall and watched the pair of us. I didn't dare look at her.

She missed something. I saw it immediately.

'Is your uncle a Roman Catholic, by any chance?' I asked, through the window of the car.

'What?' said Hammerhead.

'Is your uncle a Roman Catholic, Hammerhead?'

'Why do you ask that?' he said, looking puzzled.

'I was just wondering, that's all,' I said.

'There's nobody in my family who's a Taig,' said Hammerhead. 'You know that. There are no Taigs in my family. Are you trying to antagonize me or something? Hurry up and get in.'

'Hang on a minute,' I said. 'I just want to check something.'

'I can't believe what you've just said,' said Hammerhead, obviously reflecting on our conversation so far. 'I can't fucking believe that. You've known my mother and father all your life. You know there's no Fenian blood anywhere. We're a family of loyalists, untainted by anything.'

'I know that,' I said. 'But I was just wondering something then.'

'What's that?' asked Hammerhead.

'It's just a very small thing,' I said.

'Couldn't you tell me anyway?' said Hammerhead, who was trying to look appealing.

My mother was starting to pay attention to what we were saying. I had to lower my voice even more.

'I was wondering why there was a St Christopher in your uncle's car.'

Hammerhead saw it then. His eyes must have somehow glided past it without taking it in. A beautiful ivory carving

151

of the patron saint of travellers hanging from the rear-view mirror, where you would hang an air freshener. It was only an inch and a half tall, but I found it immediately. I don't know why I looked there, but I did. Perhaps I was looking to see what type of air freshener was in the car; the car smelt strongly of Alpine Mist, and not at all like Hammerhead or any of his untainted family.

But Hammerhead wasn't slow either. There was a pause, not a long pause, but a significant one none the less. He needed time to think, but just a little time. Hammerhead could be a quick thinker when the chips were down.

'Oh that,' said Hammerhead. 'It's my uncle's lucky charm.'

'Really,' I said.

'Well not so much a lucky charm,' said Hammerhead. 'He's in the retail business my uncle and he does a lot of work with Roman Catholics across the water, so he leaves this little lucky charm in his car to fool them, to throw them off the scent so to speak. They might not like to do business with him if they found out who his nephew was.'

He looked at me in that knowing way. We both knew what Hammerhead's cousin had done. It was his little dig at me. None of my cousins had ever done anything for Ulster. He could tell by my face that he had made his point.

'If they knew that he was related to – you know who – then they might not be so keen to deal with him. That's why he keeps it here.'

I went, 'Humppph.'

'Look, for fuck's sake get in,' said Hammerhead. 'The car's clean. You've got my word on that. I've borrowed it. Do you think that I'd be sitting here gassing away if I'd lifted it, answering all your stupid fucking questions?'

The answer told me enough. I knew he'd nicked it, but I also knew that he wanted me to go with him, and that he was so determined for me to join him that he was quite prepared to make up any ludicrous story that would do the trick. There was no backing down from situations like this for a lad from the corner. There was no way out, so I jumped in enthusiastically. I say 'enthusiastically' because it's true. We were going for a wee drive. I was in on it, so I might as well enjoy it. That's the way I looked at things.

Hammerhead had started the engine up. I noticed that he was wearing leather gloves. My mother had missed those. So had I. We both waved at my mother. She still didn't see his gloves. She looked disappointed that she wasn't coming with us. I thought Hammerhead might even suggest taking her with us. I mouthed 'Get a move on' to him. He removed the St Christopher and stuck it in his pocket. We set off towards town.

'We'd better duck when we go past the chapel,' he said. 'Better still, let's give them the fucking fingers. Up your hole with a big jam roll, you Fenian fucks,' he shouted to nobody in particular. A few seconds later we passed some men standing on the corner of some republican street. They were watching us, but Hammerhead was doing all his gesturing below the level of the window. He was not stupid.

His driving was better than I thought. He managed to keep his speed down to about fifty. The only driving test that he had ever passed was removing the car from its rightful owner in the first place. I told him that I wasn't going to lie in the back window if he crashed an army patrol. He thought that this was very funny. They called them sandbaggers, or at least the newspapers did. I had never met anybody who had ever admitted to being pushed into doing this. I had never met anybody who had ever heard the term until they read it in the papers. But the idea was always good for a laugh. We'd say to each other, 'Hey, you can be the sand-bagger tonight.' My mother didn't know what it meant. She thought it was something dirty, something sexy. We only said it for a laugh. 'Fancy being a fucking sandbagger then?'

We cruised through Holywood with the windows down, with Hammerhead giving a little wave every now and again to people on the street, until he remembered the black leather gloves. Then he told me to climb into the back window and stick my arse up against the glass to save him taking a bullet. We drove past the bungalows on the Golden Mile with the sea views, and the lights on inside in the daylight, so that we could look in with envy.

He told me that his uncle had come round the night before, to tell him about the good old days in the Organization. I asked whether the car we were in belonged to that uncle.

'Don't be fucking funny,' said Hammerhead.

'My uncle used to be one of the big operators behind Golliwog Radio,' said Hammerhead, 'the pirate radio station broadcast by the UDA in the early seventies. You must have heard about it.'

I said I hadn't.

'They used to send messages up the Falls just to irritate the Taigs. The IRA would send these messages back to irritate them on their wee pirate station. It was like two-way traffic. It sounds like great crack, playing with the radio all day. My uncle's special slot was that he used to interview this wee dog on the radio, and he used to say to it, "What do you think of Protestants?". It used to bark back, you know, *yap, yap, yap,* really friendly, licking away, all that sort of stuff. Then my uncle would say to it, "What do you think of Taigs?", and it would go fucking mad, growling down the phone, trying to bite his fucking hand off. It's just the way that they taught the wee dog to act, but it sounds like a right scream, a right good laugh.'

The traffic was slowing. For some reason Hammerhead's story made me think of wee Patrick and what he would say about David, the lad who was shot in the video shop, whenever David's name was mentioned. 'All gone.' What do you think of Protestants? *Yap, yap, yap.* You just say something and you get a response. It doesn't have to mean anything for the person, or the dog, doing it. It's the spectators, and those who organize and arrange the whole thing, who set the whole thing up, that give it its meaning. This was a depressing thought. I tried to cheer myself up by reflecting on the fact that people aren't dogs, even children aren't dogs, at least not like that. I wasn't convincing myself.

We inched past another bungalow with a man sitting on a floral chair with a high back right there in the window. He was wearing slippers and reading the paper. Hammerhead gave him a wave, which made him look up, and then the fingers. I could see him setting the paper down.

'I wonder where all his money came from,' said Hammerhead. 'My da always says that you can't earn it legally. You just can't. There are all these mugs who think you can. Mugs who go to work every day grafting away, but they're just fooling themselves. Then they come home at night, to find that somebody has fucked off with their car, and that they've been working for nothing. I like teaching them that wee lesson. It's good to be able to teach them fucking nobs something.'

We both laughed, but I couldn't say why I laughed.

'I just hope he doesn't ring the police to report you for offensive behaviour,' I said.

'What was offensive about that?' asked Hammerhead. 'I was just waving at him. Everybody waves like that up our way.'

I told Hammerhead that it was my mother's lifelong ambition to have a bungalow by the sea on the road to Bangor.

'Some fucking chance,' Hammerhead said. 'Some chance and no chance.'

Then there was a pause, with his eyes careering around inside his head. You could almost watch the trajectory of

155

Hammerhead's thoughts. It was quite eerie sometimes.

'That's not an ambition though,' he said. 'That's a dream. That's different. She's not stupid your mother. That's just her little dream. She knows that. You have to allow people to have their dreams.'

The houses now had more elaborate fronts, arches, horseshoes pinned to the wall, symmetrical tree-lined drives, red Celicas like ours out front.

'Even respectable people have to pull strokes,' said Hammerhead. 'Or get somebody else to do it for them. My uncle though makes me laugh. He drives a taxi these days. He says it's the most dangerous job in Belfast. He says he should be paid danger money. He was telling me that he got stoned on the Stonepark the night before last. They could tell it was a Protestant taxi from his sign. He forgot to take it off. I mean he laughs about it now. He just forgot. He says that the boys from up our way stone their taxis. They stone ours. It's all fair. But you should have heard him saying that he carries blind people. "Just imagine if my car had been stoned with them in it. They wouldn't have known which way to duck." He's a real hoot my uncle. Even when he doesn't mean to be.'

'I want to see the new marina down in Bangor,' I said. 'My mother tells me we won't recognize the place. Ernie told her.'

We parked in a new car park just at the end of the new marina, with a few other cars owned by the kinds of boys and girls that I went to school with. Cars given to them by their parents. Like us, they also had their windows down. I could see them looking at our car. Two more spoilt boys out for a spin on a Sunday in their brand-new Toyota. We walked out through the town, and out around the bend to smell the sea. A lough, really, with a sign saying DO NOT EAT THE SHELLFISH. DANGER POLLUTED, but it smelt of the sea and old holidays down at Pickie Pool, with the rowing boat out in the water beyond the grey pock-marked back wall of the pool with its screaming children and blue and yellow beachballs bouncing high into the sky and losing themselves in the bright sunlight. The sun always shone in those days. Hammerhead and I had played down in Pickie Pool together. But neither of us could remember it. Our parents told us about it much later. They created our days down at Pickie together for us when we were older, our long days by the seaside in glorious summer weather without end.

'Wouldn't you love to live down here with all the money people?' asked Hammerhead. 'You could wake up in the morning and go for a wee walk on the sands. You could take that half-Alsatian-half-fucking-wolf dog of yours and let it shite all over the place.'

I pointed out to him that the sand in the middle of Bangor had been filled in to make way for the new marina.

'Diabolical that. Fucking diabolical. I bet they didn't ask the people if they wanted it. I bet they didn't ask the people from Belfast who needed that wee stretch of sand if they minded. They just filled it in, to make a place for the boats for these rich cunts.'

He suggested that we walk to Ballyholme, like the old days, the old days that neither of us could remember.

We walked out along the winding path, looking at the plain Presbyterian houses. Nothing ostentatious about these. They looked dreary in the autumnal light, flat and grey against an iron-grey sky. The sea looked cold. Hammerhead said that he was going in. I told him not to bother. He stripped to his underpants and ran to the edge of the water. He dipped one toe in and ran back to his pile of clothes.

'That's it,' said Hammerhead. 'I can say that I had a swim in the middle of October in Bangor. What a man. What a fucking hero. That's me done for the day.'

He was pulling his jeans back on. He was shaking with the cold so violently that he couldn't get his left foot into the trouser leg. Then we heard a shrill whistle.

'What the fuck was that?' shouted Hammerhead.

I was ready to run and leave him there balancing on the shingle with his jeans in his hands.

The whistle sounded again. We looked up and we could just about see them on the path way up above us. Two tiny figures wrapped against the cold. One of them had her finger up near her mouth. She whistled better than I ever could.

'Hey, you with the gorgeous body,' shouted the other one.

'Our luck's in,' said Hammerhead. 'I knew it was going to be our day.'

Standing there in his grey underpants, he flexed his sinewy arms and stuck out his bony white chest. We could hear them laughing.

Then the two figures started to move off.

'Hang on a second,' shouted Hammerhead. 'We just want to talk to you.'

He slipped his jeans and shoes on and we made it up the hill. The girls had waited. I recognized her as soon as I saw her, even though she looked different. She was smiling. She was almost unrecognizable, the prettiness hidden that day in the park was out in the open.

'How's it going, girls?' asked Hammerhead. 'Do you fancy just joining two playboys down with their yacht in Bangor?'

She recognized me, but neither of us said anything. She just smiled at me; it was a gentle, inviting sort of smile. She looked happy to see me.

'Two big fucking spenders,' said Hammerhead, 'just looking for two fucking good-looking babes like you two fucking lovely girls here.' Then he seemed to remember who he was talking to. 'Sorry about the language, girls, but it's the cold,' he said. 'Two big spenders,' said Hammerhead again, this time omitting the swearing. 'In fact, two big guys in every sense of the word.'

I had not noticed her mouth that day in the park. It curled in a warm sexy way upwards at the ends. She was wearing a very pink lipstick which accentuated its shape, and blue eyeliner. She had beautiful deep coloured grey-blue eyes. Not the colourless grey I had once seen. When she turned slightly, I could see that she was wearing a lot of make-up, as if she had already got prepared for the night, and the Sunday afternoon was just a necessary interlude. She was wearing a grey fleecy duffle coat, and a short blue dungaree dress with suede boots and opaque tights. She had good legs. The clothes were for going out in really, but they would look OK as casual wear to wander around Bangor in. She was a good dresser.

'We've got the wheels ready to whisk you off your feet,' said Hammerhead, 'if you fancy coming for a wee spin that is.'

I just stood there smiling back at her, my face breaking into a long grin.

Hammerhead noticed. He nudged the other girl.

'I think these two must have met in a previous life.' he said. 'They've clicked already. I'd better do the talking because he seems to have been struck dumb. What are you doing down here, girls?'

They told us that they had come down by train, and that they just fancied getting out of Belfast for a while. It was a toss-up between Holywood and Bangor. They thought there would be more life in Bangor. You could see that they were disappointed. Hammerhead told them that they were right all along, they just hadn't found it up until now. Hammerhead suggested that we all go for a stroll, and he guided them right up to our car. They were impressed, and why wouldn't they be? Hammerhead repeated the story of his uncle over from across the water loaning the car to him for the day, and Shannon's friend seemed to fall for it.

But Shannon said, 'You haven't nicked this, have you?'

Hammerhead just laughed.

'Do you think I would park it here in broad daylight if I'd nicked it?' he said.

We all laughed as we drove along the coast, and out on to lonely winding country roads. Hammerhead asked where they wanted to go. They said they didn't mind. I said that my father used to take me fishing to Greyabbey, and that would be a good drive. Shannon just said that it sounded nice. She asked if there was an abbey there. I said I didn't know. I told her that we just went for the fishing, we never looked around when we got there.

So we set off down through the Ards Peninsula for Greyabbey, and I had a clear bright image of the roach and the rudd I used to catch in the freshwater lake there just on the other side of the road from the sea. The fish heaped in great silver twitching piles as I pulled them out of the water. And then I had this image of some country boy, younger than me, perhaps ten years old, who caught a big pike, and asked me to help him land it. I didn't see his landing net lying in the long grass, so I grabbed hold of his line and the pike just slithered off into the shallow water. It all happened very quickly. I must have pulled the line so that the hook was ripped out of the fish's mouth. My father looked at me just for a second, just for a split second, with something like embarrassment in his eyes. It was the most fleeting of looks, but I remember it. I had never seen him look embarrassed with me before.

It was as if he wanted to be proud of me for landing a big menacing pike when we were out in the country, something to tell my mother when we got back to our grey street, and I had let him down. I had spoilt it for him.

But then again I might have imagined his look. It wasn't

my fault; after all, it was a big, heavy pike, and the landing net was hidden in that long wet grass. Perhaps what I saw in my father's face was what I felt that I deserved from him. No more, no less.

But the boy's look was unmistakable. He looked at me as if I was just some stupid boy down from the city who had no idea what to do out there in the country with a pike on the line. A city boy who liked to catch a few dozen roach because they were easy, because they required no skill or effort, and hardly any bait. You could pull the hook out of one fish and leave some of its guts on, and that would do for bait for the next. It was like working in a factory, repetitive mindless action for mindless fish who didn't mind being caught and killed. One slap on your boot killed them. They didn't seem to mind, they never fought for life. They didn't struggle. Not like pike, which used all their cunning and all their sharp-toothed menace to stay alive.

The boy didn't say a word, he just shrugged. My father said something to him, and he shrugged again. I can't remember any words, just his look at me over his shoulder. I said I was sorry to the boy, but my father said that there was no need to apologize. And all the time the big pike just lay there in the shallow water, as if it was looking up at us. It was tantalizingly close. I wanted to scoop it back out with my bare hands. I had already rehearsed how we would kill it to avoid its teeth going into us. Pike have sharp teeth, I knew that. We were going to have to kill it very skilfully, without getting too close. But it lay there looking at me, as if it knew what I was thinking.

I can see its eyes now. It was staring at me, as if it knew that I was the one who had come all this way to end its life. I know it sounds ridiculous, but it looked at me as if it knew that I harboured murderous intentions towards it. But it had won in the end. It had won. That was the last time my father and I went fishing before he went into hospital with his bad

161

heart. I never got a chance to make amends. The pike would have outlived him. That was a sad depressing thought.

I drove through Greyabbey that autumn day with Hammerhead and the two girls, and I recognized nothing. All I remembered from my previous visits was that the lake was on the left and the sea was on the right. This was so clear in my mind because the pike was pointing in the direction of our car. There was a sea wall opposite the lake, and we had our sandwiches and our flask of tea behind the wall. But now we couldn't find the lake. Hammerhead was getting impatient. Shannon and her friend Lesley were bored. They were both smoking in the back. I wound my window down, and Lesley complained about the cold.

'Why did we come here, it's a dump,' said Lesley. 'Where's the abbey then?'

I told her that we weren't looking for the abbey.

'What are we looking for then?' she asked.

'A lake,' I said.

'Did something happen there?' she asked. 'Something to do with history?'

'Not much,' I said, 'but something occurred there, something significant.'

'Are there any wee reminders there?' she asked, 'any ruins or anything like that to wander around? Anything to look at?'

I told her that there might be. She'd just have to wait.

It was Hammerhead who found the lake. We had come in the wrong direction through the town. The lake was on the right. It was smaller than I remembered, with overhanging trees. No more than a pond really. We got out of the car and I found the exact spot where the pike had lain. There was a bare shiny patch on the bank after all those years. Shannon was the only one to get out of the car. She asked me if I was looking for something in particular. I said that I was. I looked into the edges of the lake with leaves wrapped around branches that had stuck in the water, where the water was gently lapping, and the trailing weeds moved in time to the soft current, and I saw the pike lying there. It had no doubt died years ago, but with that odd mixture of sea air and country air from the fields on the other side of the lake, I could see it lying there, green and silver, some scales on its back missing, teeth, sharp pointed teeth, sharp pointed head, and it was trying not to blink. It was still doing this after all those years, still remembering what I had planned to do to it. I watched that pike with my own straining eyes. I was refusing to blink in case I lost it for ever. Then I smelt him standing there. I smelt the overalls and I knew that he was there beside me. Those old overalls soaked in engine oil, oil that's worn itself deep into old cloth that's hardened. I could have reached out and touched him, but I didn't want to look round and I didn't want to blink. Then I heard him say something.

'Son,' he said.

That's all. I thought that he might say more. I thought he might tell me not to worry, or even that nobody could have seen the landing net lying in such long grass. But he didn't. That's all he said, and he said it very quietly, as if it was all a great effort.

I blinked at that point, I couldn't help it. I couldn't hold my straining eyes open any longer, and the pike darted off into the trailing weeds, and my father was torn away from me again. It was as vivid as the last bad dream before morning, the one that leaves you feeling empty inside.

I didn't want to cry and I didn't want to look at Shannon, but she could sense that there was something wrong.

'Does this place mean something to you then?' she asked.

I said that I had been there for a picnic a few times, years ago.

'Oh,' she said. 'I thought you might have had your first

163

sexual experience down here or something.' And she laughed.

'No,' I said. I tried to say it jovially. But it came out sounding like 'huh'.

Hammerhead was knocking the window of the car. He called me over. I knew what was on his mind. Lesley had got into the front beside him. I knew that look. He was showing her his swollen nose, and no doubt giving her some story about how it had happened. 'I'll have the car for a wee while, and you two can go for a walk, if that's all right?' he said.

Shannon just nodded. 'I'm easy,' she said. I didn't have to give him an answer.

'Come on, love, we'll leave these two here to gaze at each other,' said Hammerhead. 'We can go for a wee drive.'

'I'm not leaving her on her own,' said Lesley. 'He might be a fucking rapist for all I know.'

'I'll be all right,' said Shannon. 'I know this fella from round town. He's all right. He's as good as gold.'

Hammerhead and the girl with the long dark hair drove off along a narrow avenue of trees shedding the remainder of their golden autumn coat. Those last golden-brown leaves clinging to the branches, trembling in the wind, waiting to fall and die. Shannon and I walked along the shore, and found a shelter etched with lovers' names and crude carved reminders of where we were still. I could make out FUCK THE POPE carved into the seat. I didn't want her to see it. I put my hand down on top of it, and then I moved along until I was sitting on top of it. I don't know why I wanted to protect her from it. Perhaps I still had those suspicions from that day in the park, and from further back, about her being a Catholic. Perhaps I was embarrassed that someone from my own side should go to all the trouble of carving this out. All that trouble for this. We sat together staring at the grey churning sea.

164

'It's lovely to see you again, you know', she said. There was a soft humour in her voice. 'I liked you that day I saw you in the park, you know. You were so . . . gentle, compared to the rest of them.'

'How's Billy? I asked.

'I don't know,' she said. 'We had a row a couple of days ago. I think it's all over, to be honest. My mother told me it wouldn't last right from the start. Mothers know these sorts of things. Don't ask me how.

'He hit me again, you know,' she said.

She said this as if I somehow might know this already, that this might be the kind of thing that Billy and I might have spent our days discussing. Or that this was something that I would just naturally assume about Billy and his type.

She looked at me. 'You wouldn't do that to a woman, would you?'

I shook my head.

'Or any girl?'

It was as if she wanted to cover her options, to elicit a response that could never be disputed or argued about, that lent itself to no ambiguities or inflections that might change it around.

I shook my head for a second time.

'I couldn't, no,' I said.

'Are you sure?' she asked.

'I'm sure I'm sure,' I said. 'I wouldn't do that sort of thing. It's not in my nature.'

As if the things we did in passion, or in private with those we loved, were ever part of our nature, part of what we were born with rather than part of what just happened to us without the great guiding influence of nature itself.

· 'My friend Lesley took me out for the day to cheer me up. She knew that I've been very low for the past couple of days. She said she'd take me to the seaside to see the new marina. She said the sea air would do me good.

165

'Wait till you see what he did to me,' she said.

She started to rub some powder off her face just below her left eye, like a magician rubbing at his wand making things happen, and I could see a purple mark appearing, a long purple ring looping around her eye like half a monocle.

'I've had to cover it up. But you can see he gave me a right digging. You should see my shoulder. He can be a right bad pig so he can.'

She got out her make-up and a small mirror from her bag and started covering it again, as if the merest glimpse of the rawest and most naked of all flesh was all that I would ever be allowed to see. She finished covering it up and then smiled up at me.

'That's why I've had to put on so much make-up,' she said. 'I didn't want people staring at me.

'I can't believe we bumped into you today,' she said. 'That's such a coincidence. I've thought about you a lot, do you know that? You believe me, don't you?'

I told her that I did believe her. Then I told her I had thought about her. She had crossed my mind. We sat there sheltering from the wind exchanging what little we had available to make each other feel better. It was better than nothing.

'Are you going to whisk me off my feet then?' she asked. She was starting to sound like an enthusiastic child, on a Saturday morning, wanting to go to town. 'What are we going to do today?' She looked at me expectantly. 'You shouldn't have let your man take the car,' she said. 'We could have gone for a drive along the coast. You're too soft.'

'I think it's nice just sitting here talking,' I said. 'It's nice being on our own. It's hard on our street to be alone like this just watching the sea. There's always somebody who comes along and spoils it for you up our way.'

'I'm sure it's very hard up your street trying to watch the sea,' she laughed. 'You can watch those hills up there with

166

the television masts sticking out of them, but that's about all.'

I started to laugh. I liked her eyes. They sparkled when she was happy.

'Do you know how many television masts there are on Divis and Black Mountain?' I asked.

'No idea,' she said. Then she thought for a few seconds. 'Four probably? One for each channel?'

I said I wasn't sure either, so we both laughed again.

'You spend all that time up in your street with nothing to look at but television masts on those dirty green hills, and you don't even know how many there are,' she said. 'You can't be very observant.'

'I mustn't be,' I said.

We sat in silence for a few seconds, but it wasn't uncomfortable the way it might have been.

'Do you want a wee drink?' she asked. 'Lesley and I have brought something with us.' She opened her bag, and I could see down in there, among the hairbrush and the hairspray and the lipstick, three bottles of Diamond White.

'One each, and one for her when she gets back,' she said. 'She might need it. Your friend was looking at her in a certain kind of way, and I think she quite liked him.'

'Really?' I said.

'Yeah really,' she replied. 'I don't think they've gone to do a bit of bird-watching. Do you?'

I shook my head, but the truth was I wasn't sure what they had gone to do. I suppose I was surprised that her friend actually liked Hammerhead. But then, perhaps not. He hadn't had the chance yet to show what he was really like.

'Billy always told me that you were the educated one in your gang,' she said. 'Teach me something that you've learnt at school then.'

I asked her if she wanted me to do my Latin for her.

'No, not Latin – that would be too much like church – something I might understand,' she said.

I suggested poetry.

'OK,' she said. 'A wee bit of poetry.'

'Are you sure?' I asked.

'Yeah. You never know. It might turn me on,' she said. 'You never know your luck.'

I sat back on the seat, carved with names and reputations, and took a deep self-conscious breath. I wouldn't have done poetry for anybody else. I coughed theatrically.

She laughed. 'That's right,' she said. 'Get yourself geared up for it.'

'The skin, the sunburnt shade, freckles, hair,' I said. I sounded slightly breathless. I was very nervous. I thought I would try something slightly erotic, but then got worried that she might accuse me of trying to get off with her. That was one reason why I was so nervous. The other reason was that I hated my voice. Not quite like hers and not like theirs from that school of mine. Something in between, neither one thing nor another, something unheard.

She watched me carefully, almost puzzled that I was going to do some poetry for her just because she asked, and then she closed her eyes, as if she thought that is what you do when you listen to poetry. You close your eyes and you let it wash all over you, like the spray from the sea out there.

'The curious sympathy one feels when feeling with the hand the naked meat of the body.' I paused after each line to watch her face to see what she made of it. She was so quiet, it was as if she was asleep. I felt more confident because she wasn't looking at me.

'The circling rivers the breath, and breathing it in and out,
   The beauty of the waist, and thence of the hips, and thence downward toward the knees,

168

The thin red jellies within you or within me, the
bones and the marrow in the bones,
The exquisite realization of health;
O I say these are not the parts and poems of the
body only, but of the soul,
O I say now these are the soul!

'Finished,' I said, just in case she couldn't tell.

'Did you write that yourself?' she asked rubbing her eyes
as if she had just woken up from a deep sleep. 'Because it
was lovely. You sound lovely. I could have listened to you all
day. Did you write those words? Don't be embarrassed, go
on, tell me.'

I told her that I didn't write them.

'You don't have to be embarrassed, you know,' she said.
'If you wrote them, you can tell me.'

'Honest to God, I didn't write them,' I said. 'Walt Whitman
wrote them, in the middle of the last century. Not Slim
Whitman by the way, Walt Whitman.'

But the joke was lost because she hadn't heard of Slim
Whitman either. So I had to explain that I had an uncle
who loved country and western music, and that was the only
reason that I had heard of Slim Whitman. I didn't want her
to feel bad for not having heard of Slim Whitman, but she
wasn't bothered anyway.

'Oh,' she said.

'Could you not do a wee poem for me that you've written
yourself,' she said. I told her that I couldn't remember any
that I had written.

'Oh, that's a shame,' she said.

I said I could only remember the first line of one. She
told me that she wanted to hear what bits of it I could
remember.

'Turtles are lentils in my soup,' I said, then I stopped.

She exhaled sharply. 'That sounds a wee bit weird to me,'

she said. 'Billy told me that you lot were always dropping acid and E and things like that. But perhaps that poem gets a bit better when you get into it. I bet it does. Eh? You'll have to look that one up and do it for me again.'

She picked up one of the bottles. 'Can you open these bottles with your teeth, by the way, or do I need to find my bottle opener?' she said. It was as if she wanted to change the subject.

I told her that she would need the bottle opener. She tossed out the contents of her bag on to the bench.

'I should empty this bag from time to time,' she said. 'It's disgusting what's in here.'

She found the bottle opener, and opened the two bottles, and handed me one.

'Drink that slowly,' she said, 'because that's all we've got.'

I sipped the drink.

'You're not a lech like the rest of them, you know,' she said. 'That's why I like you.'

'Good,' I replied.

'But don't you fancy me at all?' she said.

I told her that I fancied her a lot.

'Thank God for that,' she said. 'I thought you might be gay for a second there. You don't look gay, but you can't tell these days.' She laughed and took a drink from the bottle. 'It's very quiet here,' she said. 'I wonder what those other two are getting up to?'

I just sighed. 'God knows,' I said.

We sat in silence. Neither of us moved. Suddenly, I could feel her hand moving, it moved up to my cheek. Slowly she moved my head around.

'Kiss me,' she said.

Her lips were soft and warm.

'Not too hard,' she said. 'We've got all day.'

I kissed her more gently.

170

'Put your tongue in,' she said, 'it'll make me wet.'

Her language startled me. I could feel my expression change, my brows furrowing as if with worry, but we were locked together so tight she could not have seen any changes. I was glad. It had just taken me by surprise, that's all. Her language excited me. I put my tongue into her mouth.

'That's lovely,' she said. 'That's fucking lovely.'

We sat there kissing for several minutes. There were some seagulls squawking above the waves, but there were no human eyes to see us. Suddenly she pulled away. I thought she had come to her senses, that guilt had made her stop. Pleasure always seemed to stop at this point in my experience. She looked at me with those big pleading eyes.

'I'm not going to let you fuck me. Do you realize that?'

I was trying not to laugh. For some reason the thought that I might go so far as to have sex with her had not entered my head. I dropped my gaze.

'Of course,' I muttered.

She touched the side of my face and moved her hand down to my chin. She tilted my head back up so that I was looking into her eyes again.

'You're not going to get a fuck. Do you understand that?'

She was waiting for an answer. I nodded slowly without looking at her.

'Good. I don't want us to get off to a bad start. It would ruin everything right at the start if you thought you were going to get something, and I had to turn you down. It would spoil everything if I had to give you the red card.'

We kissed again, or rather she kissed me. She touched the hair on my neck.

'But you're making me really wet,' she said. 'You're so gentle.'

Her hand moved down across my body until it lay on my

171

lap. She squeezed me gently. She moved her hand slowly up and down, exciting me. I could hear her breathing getting heavier, her moans deepening. She pushed me back on the seat and stood up in the shelter and took one of her boots off, then pulled her tights down off one leg. She put her boot back on quickly and then clambered into my lap. She unzipped me, and then dug her nails into it, as it stiffened in her hand. She dug her nails in so hard, it hurt. I made no sound. She slipped her black panties to one side, and sat down hard on me.

'Fuck me,' she said.

I could feel her soft wetness engulf me.

'Put your tongue in my mouth. Fucking do it,' she said.

She rocked slowly forward, and then back. She sat back quite still, looking at me, looking straight into my eyes. I could just feel this soft wetness around me, a sensation like no other. Then she rocked forward once more but even slower this time. I could feel the tightness of the elastic rubbing against me. She put her wet tongue into my mouth. As I sucked on it, I felt the surge. My hands were trying to get inside her dungarees, fumbling along the buttons. I grabbed at her buttons like a man falling off a cliff face. She let out a very deep moan.

Then there was silence. Her breaths had disappeared into some solemn void. The silence engulfed us both. I could feel the walls of the shelter throb around us. The blood was pumping in my neck. I sat in that silence for a few moments, and then I went, 'Huh' with a deep exhalation of breath, as if I couldn't think of anything to say. But I just wanted to show that I wanted the silence to stop, I wanted to show that I could take charge.

She breathed again so that I could hear her.

'Jesus Christ, you nearly bit my fucking tongue off,' she said, laughing as she climbed back off. 'It didn't take you long.'

'Have you come?' I asked.

'What?' she said. 'Are you serious? You didn't even give me time to fake it.'

She was laughing a little. I looked away. 'You haven't had much sex. I can tell that. You should have told me before we started.'

I told her that I just fancied her too much.

She laughed. 'But I can still tell that you haven't done it much before. I could have given you a wank first if you'd told me. I bet you would have liked that.'

I went very silent.

'Have you got a tissue on you? I don't want to walk about all day with this dribbling out.'

I told her that I didn't have a tissue. I said I just had a hanky. She said that the hanky would do just as long as I hadn't used it. She told me to turn round as she wiped herself. She sat back down beside me. She left her tights hanging off one leg.

I could see a boat coming up past us, a small flat vessel chugging along in the distance in the grey waters, as if it had wanted to be as far away from the shore as possible, as if it wanted to be out on its own. I didn't want to look at her. She was starting to laugh gently to herself.

'You'd better have a wank before you come out the next time I see you,' she said. 'You can't be that selfish all the time.'

I sat there thinking about all those nights dreaming of it in the flesh and this was it – on some cold morning in a grey little pebbled shelter somewhere outside Greyabbey, with a red wooden bench with names and dates and hatreds carved into it. Some freshly carved, with little red wood chippings on the seat. Somebody had been here recently perhaps for the same thing as us. I was thinking of me saying those lines of poetry to her, and her sitting with her eyes closed. I had forgotten to tell her what the poem was called. I wished

I had told her, but it was too late. It was almost a romantic prelude to the act itself.

'The armies of those I love engirth me and I engirth them.' I was remembering the other words from the poem. Perhaps I was trying to get away from the present, with her sitting there a little angry and a little frustrated. She had got the urge from somewhere and I had let her down. So she sat there with my wetness dribbling out, mopping it with my soiled hanky. She looked a little cheated.

The strangest thoughts entered my head. What would I remember about these few moments in the dark quiet hours of the years to follow? The words, hers or mine? The urgency? The hot wetness? The noise? What noise was that? It had gone already. The sensation of bristle on bone. The small quiet sounds. No noise, but the small sounds of damp bristly hair rubbing tightly on soft fleshed bone.

'I bet that was your first time,' she said with a quiet laugh. 'I bet you were a fucking virgin until two minutes ago. How old are you?' she asked.

It was almost done accusingly.

'Seventeen,' I said.

'Fucking hell,' she said. 'You're two years younger than me. I'm a fucking cradle snatcher. Why are you still a virgin though? Billy always told me that you lot were always getting your oats.'

'I'm not a virgin,' I said.

She laughed. 'Not any longer anyway.'

'I'm not,' I said.

'No, I suppose you're not. But then again that wasn't a proper fuck, you know, that wasn't proper sex. That's what you call . . .'

'Premature ejaculation,' I suggested.

'No, just crap,' she said. She was laughing very loudly now. 'Just my wee joke,' she said.

'Give us your hand then,' she said as she reached out for

me. I thought she was doing this out of affection, so I took her hand, but she just pulled me forward on the seat.

'Get on the floor,' she said. 'Kneel down in front of me, and I'll teach you what to do.'

I knelt at her feet, and she opened her legs. She grabbed my head and held me in that one position so that I couldn't move. So this was the lesson that she was going to teach me. I could feel her juices running down my chin, and I could feel myself getting hard again. She let out the sharpest yell, as if she had been stabbed in the neck, and jolted back on the wooden seat.

She pushed my head away. 'You can put your tongue away now, for fuck's sake.' I was very hard now, but I didn't know how to mention it.

'I haven't brought any spare knickers with me, and these ones are fucking soaked,' she said. 'It's your fault.' She sounded a lot happier. I was feeling relieved. She took her knickers off and put them into her bag, and then put her tights back on.

We sat in silence for a few minutes.

'Can I see you again then?' I asked. I felt I had to say something to end this newest, harshest silence.

'Of course you can. You don't think I'd just let anybody do that to me, and without a condom? You're only my second proper boyfriend. Do you know that?' she said.

'Really?' I said.

'Yeah really,' she said.

I didn't believe her, but I didn't know why she had said it. I liked the way she had taken control. I had only ever heard stories about girls resisting and fighting you off, even though they were dying for it. This was different.

'And anyway, me and Billy are finished,' she said.

She squeezed my hand. 'Just as long as your mates don't find out that you're going out with a wee Taig.'

She laughed loudly this time. I felt myself going numb. It

was slowly dawning on me what I had just done. There was a sickening feeling in the pit of my stomach. I'd just had sex with Billy's wife, my mate's wife, the mother of his wee child. I'd just had sex with a Roman Catholic, a Taig, a Fenian, a daughter of Rome. The numbness was running down my legs like the juices down hers.

She squeezed my hands harder. 'You're frozen,' she said, and then laughed again. 'That's probably another reason why it was over so quickly. You felt guilty. Or you didn't want your mate to come back and catch you half-way up a Taig.'

She fiddled with my hair. 'You know, Billy used to worry about it something rotten. I told him that you'd all have a ride if you got the chance. And today just proves it. You say you don't want anything to do with us until you're on your own with us, and then it's a different story.'

I tried a laugh; it came out like a desperate gasp.

'I didn't know you were a Catholic,' I said. 'Billy never told any of us. He didn't exactly broadcast it.'

'Do you like the taste of forbidden fruit then?' she asked. She kissed me again. 'Have you seen anything of that no-good husband of mine, by the way? I suppose he's moved back in with his family?'

I told her I had seen him at the corner.

'That chip shop, where he used to stand with the rest of his no-good pals? I'm not talking about you, I'm talking about the rest of them. He used to go on about it, as if it was some place. It's fucking nowhere. It's just a greasy fucking chip shop where nothing ever happens.'

I nodded my head. 'It's just somewhere to hang about,' I said. 'Just somewhere for us to be.'

'I've moved back in with my mother,' she told me. 'Do you know where Smithwick Street is?'

I shook my head.

'I didn't think you would. I bet you've never been up there before. It's off the Falls. How do you feel about visiting me up there? That would be a wee test for you, to see how much you like me. I'll have to draw you a wee map otherwise you'll get lost. We can't have you wandering about the Falls asking for Smithwick Street. They'd think you were some mad loyalist bomber who's got lost.'

She got a cigarette packet out of the pocket of her coat and pulled out her last cigarette, and lit it. She flattened out the box and started to draw with a blue eyeliner. 'I'll see you tomorrow night. Yeah? Do you want me to write the day and the time on as well, or do you think you could remember those yourself?'

Just then I heard a car shuddering along the road. I looked up and could see that Lesley was driving the Celica back.

'Holy fuck, here's your friend back again. He didn't go far. It's just as well we got a move on.'

The car pulled up on the main road. I could see Hammerhead leaning over and tooting the horn. Lesley came running down. By the time she got to the shelter she was out of breath.

'He says the two of you have to get off now,' she said gulping the air. 'He says that his uncle is expecting his car back. That's a lovely wee car by the way. He let me drive back.'

We drove back to Bangor in silence. The two girls were in the back again. We let them off at the marina. We all got out to look at the boats. But Hammerhead said that we had to go after a couple of minutes. Lesley touched my sleeve. 'It was lovely meeting you. I'm sorry we didn't get a chance to talk more.'

I smiled.

'Shannon and I are here for the whole day,' she said. 'We're going out for a meal in Bangor tonight.'

I checked that the cigarette box was still safe in my pocket and walked over and kissed Shannon on the cheek.

'It was lovely meeting you,' I said.

She winked at me. 'See you around,' she said. She turned to Lesley. 'I thought this guy was the fella from Cheechie's, but it wasn't him at all. He's the spitting image of him.'

'He looks like a lot of people,' said Lesley. 'He's got that type of face.'

Hammerhead just nodded at the two girls. 'See you around,' he said.

I got in beside Hammerhead and he roared off. He was speeding away from the hills over the sea, and the flat grey houses of that Presbyterian coast. He didn't say anything for a few minutes. He was waiting for me to say something.

'Well?' he said eventually.

'Well what?'

'Did you get anything?'

'No,' I said.

'Neither did I,' he said. 'But do you want to know the truth?' he asked.

'Tell me,' I said.

'I didn't want anything. 'Do you want to know why?'

'Why?' I asked.

'Because,' he extended the second syllable of this word so far he was able to go round a busy roundabout with the one word. 'I think they were a pair of wee Taigs, that's why.' The sentence had speeded up as he had gone through it. 'Wee Taigs' came out sounding like just one syllable. 'I'm not kidding you, a pair of wee fucking Taigs.' The syllables ran into each other, as if the first syllable was gobbling up the rest.

'Baaaalicks,' I said. I knew how to extend sounds for maximum effect as well. 'Fucking baaaaaaaalicks.'

'Do you know why I think that?' asked Hammerhead after a silence which had started to feel oppressive between us.

'Why?' I said.

'I hung that St Christopher back up in the car when she wasn't looking and she noticed it immediately. She saw it and she thought it was lovely. She was sitting there admiring the fucking thing.'

Hammerhead's face was set in a hard exaggerated expression of disbelief, a look of utter incredulity. 'She sat there, God be my witness, admiring the fucking thing.'

He was driving faster.

'Slow down for fuck's sake,' I said. 'We don't want to get pulled. Drive carefully for fuck's sakes.'

'She thought we were a couple of Fenians,' said Hammerhead. 'Do you know that? I hope you didn't tell them our names, because I played along with it. I told her we lived up on Hillview Road with the rest of the nationalists, and that we were hemmed in all the time because of those bastard Prods down at the corner. I had a good laugh to myself because she was nodding away in agreement and saying how awful it must be living up there.'

'But the funniest thing is,' said Hammerhead, as we pulled out on to the road to Holywood, 'is that she left her prints all over the car. Along with yours of course. But you can give your bit of the car a wee wipe before you get out. But if she's ever been in trouble before and they've got her prints on file, she'll be up shit creek now without a paddle.' Hammerhead was laughing away. 'As soon as I twigged that she was a Taig, I asked her if she fancied a drive of the car. I could have laughed my baaaalicks off as I watched her put her sweaty little hands all over the steering wheel.'

He glanced over at me. I wasn't laughing.

'Cheer up for fuck's sake,' Hammerhead said. 'It's just a fucking nobble. Slap it up the wee Fenian bitches. That's what I say.'

We roared past the big houses on the Golden Mile. Hammerhead couldn't even be bothered waving now.

'But do you want to know the truth?' asked Hammerhead. 'If I knew where either of them lived, I'd dump this car outside her house. That would be a right fucking laugh. You

179

don't know either of their addresses, by any chance, do you?'

I shook my head.

'It's a pity that,' said Hammerhead. 'Or we could have had a right laugh stitching up a couple of Taigs, framing them for joyriding. The Provos might have even been round to their house with a few wee lessons for them, especially because a . . .'

And he paused. He looked round at me. 'Are you ready for this, smart fuck? Are you ready for a bit of a sensation?'

I told him to get on with it.

'Especially because a priest owns this here car. His collar was on the back seat. Honest to God! You couldn't make it up if you tried. A priest with a brand-new red Celica! The Provos would be round at those girls' houses tonight, if they found out, because you know how forgiving priests can be.'

Hammerhead was laughing almost hysterically.

'You don't know any numbers that you can ring up to tip the IRA off about anti-social elements in their community? A number like that would come in handy at times like this.'

He was still laughing when he dropped me off at my front door.

11

She could tell that I was going out to see somebody, somebody special. I was never that careful with my personal hygiene. I was always clean, but I had asked her where the talcum powder was. That was the give-away. Who uses talcum powder if they're not expecting to have sex? She asked me several times who it was I was going to see. I told her that I was going to a club in the city. She said, 'On a Monday? Nobody goes out on a Monday except whores and whoremasters.' I said that this might have been true in her day, but not now. I told her that I didn't know when I would be back. She asked me again who I was going to the club with. I said that it was Tucker. I told Tucker not to call round that night. He loaned me twenty quid.

When I say that he loaned me the money, he knew I had no way of paying him back. He gave me twenty quid. I told him that I'd pulled. A girl from my school, a girl from the Antrim Road. 'She'll expect you to spend some money on her then,' said Tucker. I was only expecting ten, but he gave me twenty, and told me to have a good time. I was lying to everyone. That's not good. You end up trying to cover yourself on all sides.

I couldn't get a taxi from my house across town and up the Falls, because this would be an event so newsworthy that everyone would get to hear about it. There was also the minor problem that no taxi driver from up our way would do such a run. It would be too dangerous. So it was a black cab into town and a long walk. Shannon had anticipated this because the map started from just above the Royal. She knew I would be walking. For once I didn't think of my father, my mind was on the present, even when I saw the outline of that red-brick building towering up in front of me.

It was a wet misty night, damp seeping through my clothes. I'd never been up that road before. Perhaps when I was young, in the car with my father. Perhaps then, but not since. I thought to myself that if I just kept my head down and acted natural I would be OK. Divis Street was deserted, which helped. I saw almost nobody as I walked up the Falls, until I got to near Beechmount Avenue. I knew that it was Beechmount Avenue, because I could see the mural from a distance. I knew that mural from the news, the *News at Ten*, a good backdrop for tales of republican violence. I could almost hear Big Ben striking when I saw the painting on the gable wall.

There was a gang of lads standing below it, about five of them. Young lads, the kind of lads who knocked about the corner, lads like us really. But they were Catholic. That was probably the only difference. But I didn't like to think about that. I kept my head down, praying they wouldn't say anything to me. I could see them watching, trying to see if they knew me. They waited until I got right up to them.

'Hey,' one of them said.

I walked on, but I could feel my steps shortening. It's almost automatic that. I knew they wouldn't give up and that I would have to stop. My steps got shorter and shorter.

'Hey you,' he said again.

I stopped just by them, and looked round at them.

'What do you want?' I said. I tried to make it as casual as possible. I tried to make the words run into each other the way that you do. Casual but friendly. It came out sounding

182

defensive, full of staccato rhythms. I could hear my own voice as if I was some distance away from it, as if it didn't really belong to me. It sounded very strange.

'Do I know you?' said the one who had shouted. They all stood in a line, scrutinizing me standing there, pallid in the glow of the streetlight, whiter than normal. I tried a smile. It felt tight. I could feel my gums as if my teeth had retracted into them, the way your balls hide in your body when you're frightened. My teeth seemed to have gone up into my gums. My lips wouldn't move the way they should. I was grimacing. I didn't answer. I just stood there grimacing, trying to smile, getting paler. I hoped they wouldn't notice.

'I know him,' said the tall thin one standing beside the one who had called out to me. 'It's Marty's mate. I fucking know him. He lives down in Calico Street in the house with the brown door. The one with the fucking handle always hanging off. Number thirty-nine. That's it. Thirty-nine. I know this guy.'

'Oh that house,' said the one whose call had stopped me. 'The house with the brown door and no handle.' He laughed. 'I don't even know what house you're talking about. I don't even know Calico Street.'

'What's his name?' said the thin one to nobody in particular. 'Um, don't fucking tell me. Ah . . .'

I stood there, trying to stop my leg shaking from the cold and the fear. I was in a dilemma. Should I agree with whatever name he came up with? What would happen if he wanted to revise it? Would I agree with the revision? Should I make up my own and disagree with whatever he said? These thoughts flashed through my head, leaving little visual traces. I could almost see the traces of the thoughts, like tracer in a night sky, criss-crossing each other, going nowhere. My last thought was that the brain can process a lot of information when it has to, most of it quite fucking useless.

'Ah fuck! What's his name?' said this tall thin lad. He was

stamping his foot in frustration. 'What's his fucking name?' He was talking about me as if I wasn't there.

He started punching the gable wall.

'Tell us your name, fuckhead, and put Gerry here out of his misery,' said a shorter squat lad with a shaved head beside him. 'Fucking get it over with.'

'Let him try to remember,' I said, 'it'll be good for him.' I didn't know where these words came from. They just came out without me deliberately planning what I was going to say. I was thankful.

They all laughed.

'I've got it. It's Brian, Brian fucking O'Neill. That's it, isn't it? Brian fucking O'Neill. You used to go to St John's. Isn't that right? You were in the same class as Sean Smith. The two of you were always in trouble.'

I stood there in silence. He hadn't just suggested a name for me. He had offered me a partial biography.

'I know this guy,' he said. 'I fucking know him. It's Brian O'Neill.'

'He's been struck dumb,' said the squat one with the shaved head. 'You've found him out. He didn't realize you were going to drag up his past as well.'

They were all laughing.

'You can't go anywhere without being recognized,' I said. 'That's the trouble with Belfast. It's such a wee place.'

'You were a fucking headcase,' said the thin one again. 'Do you remember you used to do those animal noises in class? Some of the teachers thought you should be in an institution. Do some for us now. Go on, do your noises for us.'

'Go on,' said the squat one, 'let's hear your animal noises. Do your fucking party piece for us then.'

I stood there, praying that they would give me a clue as to what kinds of animal noises they were talking about – farmyard animals? Domestic animals? Wild animals? Elephants? Badgers? What kinds of fucking animals?

'Hurry up,' said the thin one. 'Do the noises. Give us all a fucking laugh. Do the fucking seal. I loved that one.'

As soon as he said the word 'seal', I could feel my heart lifting.

I coughed and made a whooshing noise like a seal coming to the surface.

'That sounds more like a fucking owl,' said the squat one.

'I haven't finished yet, give us a chance,' I said.

I did it louder this time, as if my life depended on it. I did some actions as well, a seal flapping, an old female seal stranded on the beach. I hopped up and down Beechmount Avenue like a seal that had been clubbed by a hunter, bleeding, dying in the Arctic wastes, trying to make its way to its mate, buffeted by the freezing winds of the North Pole.

When I stopped, I looked at them. I swear that their mouths were hanging open. Then the thin one burst out laughing, then they all did, as if taking their cue from him.

'I told you he was good,' he said. 'He used to do that in class all the time. What a fucking laugh.'

They were all laughing, it was genuine laughter. I heard the squat one saying, 'I can understand why some of the teachers thought he should be in an institution. He's a fucking nutcase.'

I asked them whether they wanted my elephant now. They didn't answer. But I held my trunk out in front of me and charged up and down Beechmount Avenue, the name changed on the gable wall to RPG Avenue, Rocket-Propelled Grenade Avenue. I ran up and down this street, this very seat of militant republicanism, acting like a bull elephant in heat. I mounted the streetlamp and I fucked that. I mounted a postbox and had simulated sex with that as well. I was an elephant and I was rampant. My heart was pounding. I was in heat but in reality I was very, very frightened.

'I've never seen that one before,' said the thin one.

'He's definitely a fucking nutter,' said the squat one, much more loudly this time. 'He should be in Purdysburn. I think we should ring for an ambulance. Does anybody here know the number?'

I stood sweating, and out of breath. It was a cold damp night, but I could feel the sweat trickling down inside my shirt.

'How's your mother?' said the thin one in a warm tone. 'How's she keeping?'

I said that she was fine in a nonchalant, easygoing sort of way.

'I thought she was terminally ill,' he said. 'Hasn't she got cancer? My ma told me that she was dying. My ma told me that she was at death's fucking door the last thing she fucking heard. How can you say that she's fine?'

'I mean that she's fine for somebody with cancer,' I said. 'As fine as can be expected is what I meant to say. I mean that she's not dead yet, which is pretty fine, for somebody who is dying.'

The squat one was throwing looks at his friends, as if to say, Get this fucking nutcase out of here. He's lowering the tone of the place. His friends were obviously receptive to this channel of communication.

'Well,' said the thin one, 'we'll see you around. Eh? Give my regards to your mother. Keep doing the animal noises. They're a good laugh. That's what Belfast needs – more comedians on the streets.'

'Do you want me to do my IRA impression now?' I asked.

There was a silence. I felt as if I had got a bit carried away, as if I had pushed my luck a little too far.

'I can do an IRA man stuck in Bellevue Zoo with a tiger if you like? An IRA man half-way up a tiger's arse.'

'No, it's all right, honest,' said the thin lad, 'you're a gas, honest to God, we've seen enough. We'll see you around.'

I could hear the murmur of talk, as I walked off. They

sounded relieved that I was going. The sweat was trickling down my sides. I wiped it off my brow. Smithwick Street was only three streets away. I didn't dare get the map out again. I stood at the corner of Smithwick Street and opened my coat, and pulled up my shirt and dried the sweat with my hanky. I thought about that day in the shelter outside Grey-abbey, and what Shannon had done with the hanky. The thought disgusted me. If I hadn't been so far away from home, I might have turned back. I walked up Smithwick Street. I remembered the number from an earlier look at the map. I knocked on her door. They had a proper knocker, not like our house where you had to pummel the wood itself, but their knocker was rusty. A woman in her late forties answered the door. She had a tired grey face. But there was a certain kindness about it. She was wearing slippers in the shape of black-and-white rabbits.

'Yes?' she said.

'Is Shannon in?' I asked.

'She's out, love. I'm sorry.'

'Oh,' I said.

'Do you have any idea when she might be in?' I enquired.

'I'm sorry love, I don't.'

There was a silence, as we both stood there looking past the door at each other. I glanced down at her slippers. They made me feel safe. I don't know why.

'Oh,' I said.

'Who is it?' said a man's voice from the front room.

'It's James,' I shouted in. 'I've come to see Shannon.'

'She's just gone up to her sister's, James. She'll be back in about half an hour,' he shouted. 'She told me to tell you this, *if* you called.' There was a lot of emphasis on the 'if', as if my calling was somehow in doubt.

'Do you want to come back in half an hour?' said the woman. 'I'm her mother, by the way. They call me Alex.'

The thought of wandering around Smithwick Street and

187

RPG Avenue for half an hour, having already performed my animal noises, filled me with the greatest dread possible. It must have shown.

'Or you can come in, if you want,' said Shannon's mother.

'Thank you very much,' I said, as I followed her into the living room.

There was a young man of about twenty sitting in an armchair. He nodded over at me, but turned back to the television almost immediately.

'Shannon said that some guy might be popping round. Do you live local?' he asked. 'I'm her brother Lenny.'

'Calico Street,' I said. 'Number thirty-nine.'

'Oh, are you Mary O'Neill's son?' asked Shannon's mother. 'I didn't know her son was called James.' She sounded very surprised, as if she should have recognized me. I had now adopted a new hybrid name to survive up in West Belfast that night.

'That's right,' I said. 'I am Mary's son. Do you know my mother?'

'Know her?' she said. 'We went to school together. How is your mother keeping?'

I was just about to answer, when her expression changed completely.

'Oh, I'm really sorry, she passed away last week. Didn't she? It slipped my mind. Oh. I'm sure it was terrible. I'm really sorry that I brought it up. You must be feeling awful. It's so stupid of me.'

I nodded. Or rather it was a cross between a nod and a shake.

'It was terrible,' I said after a few moments where I composed myself. 'But the end was quick.'

'I'm pleased you can look at it that way,' said Shannon's mother. 'Three days of agony sounds hellishly slow to me.' She looked at me.

'But it's quicker than usual,' I said. 'With that type of

188

cancer it's usually slower than that. It's usually more like five days. She had one of the quicker ones.'

'Oh,' she said.

She went in to make some tea.

'Are you seeing Shannon then?' said Lenny.

'Sort of,' I said.

'She's married, you know,' he said, 'with a wee one. He's upstairs asleep.'

'I know,' I said. 'She told me all about it.'

'It was a mixed marriage,' said Lenny. 'Did she tell you that? It didn't work out. They never do. Thank God she's seeing one of her own.'

I went, 'Yeah.'

Lenny started to get up out of his chair. He reached for some crutches. He saw me looking over at him, but he said nothing. He mounted the stairs with great difficulty. I could hear him heaving himself up, using the crutches as a lever. Shannon's mother came back in with the tea. She saw me watching Lenny.

'He had an accident,' she said. 'A serious one. He's on crutches, he will be all his life.'

I could see her eyes watering, as if some dust had been blown into the corner of her eye, but she controlled it well.

'How long have you known our Shannon then?' she asked.

I went, 'Um' to give me time to think. I heard the front door opening, and Shannon walked in. I was relieved not to have to tell any more lies. She looked surprised to see me. She burst out laughing.

'Well, well, well. You're reliable, I'll give you that,' she said. 'I just had to go round to my sister's. For some reason I thought you'd be a bit late.'

She went upstairs to get dressed, leaving me and the mother in front of the television. I pretended to be interested in the prizes on the game show. We spent our time together discussing the prizes. Shannon came down the stairs dressed up, ready to go out. She looked happy.

We got a taxi into town. The driver knew her. I could tell by the way he nodded to her. There was something in it, some affection. I could see him looking at me in his mirror, trying to work out who I was. I told Shannon all about my ordeal at the corner of Beechmount Avenue, and she laughed. I whispered the story to her in the back of the cab. She held my arm and laughed into the torn back seat of the taxi.

'You take some chances,' she said.

The driver gave us a discount. He gave us a price and then knocked fifty pence off.

She took me to a club that I hadn't been to before, right in the centre of town. We got into a queue. I noticed that the doormen had little earpieces in their right ear, and a microphone on their shirt. The microphones were flesh-coloured, and looked curiously like something from the National Health Service, the colour of cheap prostheses. One doorman was having trouble working his. 'You have to put your head right down into your chest,' said his friend. 'You can't just stand there and talk normally.'

'I can hear fuck all in this,' said the first.

The queue edged its way towards them.

'I think mine's not working,' said the first; 'can we do a wee test?'

So they stood there in the entrance to this club, three feet apart, talking to each other through their earpieces to see if their state-of-the-art security system was working.

I nudged Shannon, thinking that she might laugh, but she just gave a short smile, before she said hello to them both. They smiled back, and glanced at me in an inquisitive sort of way. She obviously knew the bouncers and they let us in for nothing. I could feel them looking at me as I walked in, trying to work out who I was and what our relationship was. She was showing me around, like a boy up from the country. She told me that a lot of English businessmen over on business in Belfast went to this particular club.

'It's the top spot,' she said. 'But they're only looking for one thing.'

'That's what the doormen tell me anyway,' she added after a momentary pause.

The club was very dark inside, the colours were black and gold, which made the whole place look even darker. The dance floor was quite small. I noticed that quite a few of the men were middle-aged. They just stood around watching a couple of girls on the dance floor. Some of the girls looked a bit rougher than I had expected for a club like that, and I thought they probably knew the bouncers as well. The drinks were very expensive. There was a black guy behind the bar with a white bow tie and a black shirt. I had never seen a black guy behind a bar before. There weren't any blacks up our way. He had a big white smile. He smiled a lot, especially when he was telling you the price of the drinks. I think he thought it was funny. We sat in a dark corner kissing, and she put my hand on her thigh. I could feel the warm soft flesh. She was wearing hold-ups. She made low moaning noises as I stroked her. Shannon and I talked and she told me about her family but she never mentioned her brother's accident. In the end, I brought it up, but she said that she didn't want to talk about it. She bought every other drink, which was just as well.

When she went to the toilet, I could hear two other bouncers talking. One was saying that his wife was like Sherlock Holmes. 'She checks my car every morning,' he said. 'She can find a single pubic hair. She's incredible. But I take the dogs out in my car. I tell her they're dog hairs. But she can tell them apart. She should join the RUC.'

I was hoping they would have finished this conversation

before Shannon got back. I didn't want either of us to be embarrassed, just in case she had ever left any traces of herself on some dark night in the back of a car where dogs sometimes lay. I didn't want something like that to ruin our mood, so delicately constructed in that dark, smoky place. But it was funny being in that club with her for the whole evening. I felt comfortable with her that night, more comfortable than I had ever felt with anybody before, and I knew then that she was something special. Too good for this club, and if the truth be known too good for most of Belfast. There were many things that we couldn't talk about – Billy, her brother, her street, my street, the future. But she held me close, and the bouncers with their tales of wives hunting for pubic hairs on the back seats of cars seemed distant and foreign and nothing to do with us. She held my hand and her eyes sparkled, and I could see no further than those bright jewels in front of me that glinted from every angle. I was happy.

When we left the club, we stood in front of the Europa waiting for a taxi. They were all busy, even on a Monday night, hailed by clubgoers standing in the middle of the street. She told me that's what I would have to do if I wanted a cab.

'You can't be too soft, or people will trample all over you,' she said.

Finally, some man in an unmarked car drove up and asked us whether we were looking for a cab. He wasn't a proper taxi, but he said he would give her a lift home. We had already agreed that there was no point in me trying to go home with her. I watched her get into the guy's car, I caught a glimpse of her bare thigh. I could see the driver looking as well. She kissed me good-night, and told me to ring her at her sister's. I could see the driver watching her all the time. He had ginger hair and a little ginger goatee. That's about all I noticed. I asked her whether she would be all right. She said she knew how to handle men, and she recognized this particular guy. I watched them drive off, and for a few seconds I felt quite lonely standing there in the middle of town, like a jilted lover, standing on the street. It was an odd feeling.

I walked up through Smithfield in the cold night air. I thought of old Joe Kavanagh's shop, I BUY ANYTHING, when he used to have the old daggers and bayonets in the window, and I would go down on a Saturday afternoon to stare at the old clocks and watches. I finally caught a taxi half-way up the Shankill. It just pulled up beside me. I didn't even have to wave it down in the end. I was back on my home turf. I felt safe and happy. I had used my wits and survived out there in territory I didn't know – survived behind enemy lines. I sat in the back of the cab smelling her skin from the tips of my fingers, coaxing myself to believe that it had not all been a glorious dream. The driver was whistling at that time in the morning. I felt like joining him. But I didn't know the tune. He was happy, and I was pleased. He let me off outside my house, and told me to look after myself. When he drove out of our street, the street descended into darkness. One of the streetlights had gone out, or perhaps Kingo's da had had it put out, to show who was boss. I was remembering the story my mother had told me. I didn't know whether to believe it or not. I was sure that these lights went out by themselves. But when the taxi drove off, the street went very dark, as if somebody had thrown a switch.

Then I noticed it. There was a car up on the far side of the road outside Mr McMurray's house. That was unusual. Mr McMurray didn't have a car. I could see it in the moonlight. I thought that it was empty at first, but when I looked more carefully I could see three or four men in it, at half-two in the morning. I was looking at it, my eyes straining, trying to see into it from that distance when the doors of the car sprang open – front and back. I turned away to get the key

193

into the door. I could hear the *click-clack* of some shoes on our street. The key wouldn't go in. I looked round quickly – just a glance – and I saw them, three of them in balaclavas striding towards me, fanning out. I could see a gun. It glinted. It was as simple as that. It was small but it had a shiny barrel and it glinted in what little light there was in the street. It might have been from the light of the moon, I don't know. I didn't think that guns really glinted, but they do. They seem to attract light. It's the first thing you notice – something shiny like that. I could feel the blood pump in my head. I remember saying, 'Jesus' out loud. The key wouldn't turn. Our lock needed a wee bit of oil, it never worked first time. I remembered that. I'd forgotten to oil it. I could hear them running. The door wouldn't open. They were right up to me. I could feel my shoulders turning inwards. I was still trying to turn the key. I could feel the pulse thumping in my neck. I thought I might pass out with the pressure of the blood pumping around my body. I sank to my knees, and covered my head with my arms. I didn't want it in the head, this seemed instinctive.

'Get up,' said one of the hooded men. 'Get up on to your fucking feet.' I lay there, scrunched up, refusing to move. I could feel my heart beating right through my chest, like a bass drum reaching some orchestral climax. I kept my arms up over my head. I was making a whimpering sort of noise. It was a funny noise, a bit like a puppy. I'd never made that noise before, or since. 'Get fucking up,' the voice said again. 'It's me. It's Tucker.'

I looked up to see Tucker removing his balaclava. He was starting to laugh.

'Well, you've shit yourself for a start,' he said.

The other two were laughing as well.

I rose to my feet slowly.

I couldn't talk, my heart was pounding. I took a deep breath.

194

'Who are your friends?' I asked. My voice sounded breathless. The shallow breath hardly got me to the end of the question.

'You don't need to know,' said Tucker. 'These are just two guys sent out as part of the hit team. You don't know them, and it's better if you don't see their faces.

'Better for you, better for them, better for me as well, I suppose,' he said, like a man out following orders, but trying to sound like a free and rational agent.

The two hooded men were still both laughing.

'He thought he was going to get a head job,' said the bigger of the two, 'let's check his pants to see if he's shat himself.'

'I haven't fucking shit myself,' I said. 'You just took me by surprise, that's all. I've never shit myself.'

'Prove it,' said the hooded man. 'Drop your fucking trousers and prove it. Prove to me that you haven't shit yourself at this very point in time.'

'Fuck off,' I said. 'You go and drop your own trousers and let's see what's in there.'

Tucker had to intervene. 'That's enough of that. It's not you that we're here to see. It's Hammerhead. You'll never guess what he's been up to.'

'What?' I asked.

'He's been joyriding. And that's not all. Before he dumped the car he hit somebody at a zebra crossing.'

What little colour I had, on that cold night on the street with one of the lights off, left me. I could feel my body going limp. It may have been delayed shock, but I don't think it was.

'But you'll never guess who he hit on the crossing,' said Tucker.

'Who?' I said.

'Big Phil's father-in-law. That's who,' said Tucker. 'Hammerhead is in deep trouble. Deep, deep trouble.'

195

The hooded man to Tucker's right was just nodding his head.

'Deep fucking trouble, if you know what we're talking about,' he said.

I said that I could imagine what he was talking about.

'Deep shit,' he said, just in case I couldn't.

'And that's not all,' said Tucker. 'Some silly cunt was with him in the car.'

Tucker's eyes were on me. I felt naked in front of him. My right leg trembled.

'You see, Big Phil's wife was down in Bangor for the day. She goes down there every Sunday to take their wee dog for a walk on the beach, or what used to be the beach before they concreted it over. She saw the pair of them. She's not sure who the other guy was, they were driving quite quickly, but Hammerhead wasn't on his own. That's for definite. But he was on his own when he hit Big Phil's father-in-law, so we're going after him first. That's our orders. The other one can wait for a while.'

'How does this concern me?' I asked, trying to control my voice.

'Well if we call for him, he's not likely to come out is he?' said Tucker. His two companions laughed again. 'Especially after our little altercation at the corner the other night. But he likes you. He trusts you. You're very plausible. I've heard your mother saying that, and it's true. You're a plausible wee shite. We just want you to call for him and then we'll have a word with him to make sure that he doesn't behave so recklessly in his home community again. As Big Phil says, if we can't show that we can police our own community, who's going to give us any respect?'

I begged Tucker to consider what he was planning to do. But he just said that he had his orders, and his two companions were with him to make sure that he could follow orders correctly.

196

'It's not up to me,' he said. 'I've been given my instructions. There's no room for manoeuvre here. I have to do what I'm told, and you have to do what you're told.'

I asked him if I went and begged Big Phil whether it would make any difference.

'It's nothing to do with Big Phil as such. He's only a little cog as well. We're all just little cogs in a bigger wheel following orders. Hammerhead broke the rules, now he has to suffer the consequences. We can't negotiate on this one.'

They walked with me round the next street to Hammerhead's house. I had trouble dragging my legs there, but every time I slowed down, one of the men in the balaclavas nudged me gently as if to remind me to keep going. I knocked at Hammerhead's door quietly three times with the palm of my hand, not with my knuckles. I was hoping that nobody would hear. There was no answer. I looked at them imploringly.

'Can we leave it?' I asked. Nobody answered.

Just then Hammerhead's mother came to the door.

'Is Thomas in, Mrs Wilkinson?' I asked.

'What do you want with him at this time of the night? Get off to bed with you. Do you know what time it is?'

I told her that it was urgent, that I just had to see him. Hammerhead had heard the knocking, he came down the stairs with just his jeans on, his bushy ginger hair was all over the place. His mother went back to bed.

'Are you all right?' he said to me. He looked genuinely concerned. This made it all that much worse. I didn't answer. I just nodded behind me. Tucker and his two new friends just grabbed Hammerhead and pulled him out of his hall. One stuck some tape over his mouth, the other put some tape around his wrists pulled round behind his back. They dragged him backwards down the street and up the entry. Tucker was the one left holding the gun.

'I'm going to cut this short,' said Tucker. 'I'm here on

197

active service on orders of the North Belfast Brigade of the UDA to punish you for anti-social activities against the Protestant people of our area. I was going to interrogate you about your fucking joyriding trip, but it's too cold for all that. So I just want to get it over with. You know why we're here, and we know why we're here, so you're just going to have to take your punishment like a man.'

Tucker had rehearsed most of these words. I could tell. They came out too quickly. There were no pauses. They sounded like somebody else talking. He wanted to say it all quickly before he had time to think, to get it over with.

'He needs to be face-down on the ground,' said the larger of the two hooded men. 'Face-down.'

Hammerhead was desperately trying to stay on his feet. One of the hoods kicked his feet away from him so that he fell backwards. They then rolled him over on to his face. As he rolled I saw that look of fear in his face and bewilderment. He looked up at me. He couldn't understand what I was doing there. They got him face down, and were trying to pull his legs straight. There were loose stones and chippings stuck into the white skin on his back.

Tucker stood astride him.

'Get the gun a bit closer. You don't want to miss him for fuck's sake,' said the smaller of the two hooded men. 'That's it now. That's about the right distance. Go on, let him fucking have it.'

I looked away, I looked up at the yard wall and the broken glass jutting out of the top of the wall. Sharp jagged silhouettes in the sky. I listened to a cat screech and wail. There was a long silent pause in the dark shadows of the entry. Even the cats seemed to be silent. I thought that Tucker was like an apprentice laying his first cable, or replacing his first oil filter. He was standing there following his gaffer's instructions. Right until the last minute I thought nothing would happen. Hammerhead had been a bit out of line, so had I. He needed a scare. Nothing more. Suddenly, there was a deafening roar. Tucker had fired. The noise was deafening in the entry. All the life that lived in that entry scurried away from that bright noisy flash. I could hear Hammerhead's body jolt across the loose stones in the entry.

'Once more for good measure,' said the smaller man again.

Tucker hesitated then fired for a second time, and I could hear a long low muffled wail from a twisting, turning white slab of body lying on the ground, which shuddered and jolted as a second bullet drove its way in through the joint of his leg, shattering his kneecap.

'Job done,' said the bigger of the hooded men. 'Let's get back to the car.'

I knew that I was crying, even though I could not feel any tears. I could see Hammerhead, Tucker and me up the glen one summer afternoon climbing trees. Hammerhead was stuck in the branches, not able to get down, but still laughing. Tucker and I were throwing sticks at him. But now he was lying there in the entry, his back splattered with bits of tarmac, this low thin moan coming from beneath the tape. I thought of him and Tucker at my father's funeral. Hammerhead looking down at his shoes because he couldn't bear to look me in the face.

'Can I untie him?' I asked.

'Leave him,' said the smaller hooded man. 'His mother can do that. That's what mothers are for. You go home now, and keep your mouth tightly fucking shut.'

I looked over at Tucker. I could see the streaks on his face, and there was no rain that night. No rain anywhere, and I knew then instantly that orders from above and distributed power are evil, evil fucking ideas, and that the problem with the Organization was that it allowed orders to be given and orders to be followed, and that nobody in the end would be really responsible for that man writhing on the ground in front of us, who would never ever walk again properly. Tucker seemed to have trouble controlling himself. Suddenly, and without warning, the smaller of the two men in the balaclavas burst out laughing.

'We had you going tonight, and this cunt at our feet,' he said. 'He was only firing blanks for fuck's sake. Tucker didn't know that, mind. It was just a warning for fuckbrain here, and a wee test for Tucker. Next time fuckbrain decides to go joyriding, it'll be the real thing. Big Phil's father-in-law wasn't badly hurt, in fact Hammerhead didn't actually hit him. He nearly did though. If he had hit him, this would have been for real.'

The two men in the balaclavas were both laughing as Tucker stood there shaking. He had never fired a gun before, and he thought he had just crippled one of his oldest friends. Hammerhead's body had jolted when it heard the gun fire, it was just an instinctive reaction.

'Untie the cunt, and get him into the house,' said the smaller hooded man. 'He'll need a sit down.'

'And some toilet paper probably,' said the other one as they walked back up the entry, taking Tucker with them.

I stood there watching them until they were out of sight. Then I pulled the tape off Hammerhead's mouth and the tape from round his wrists and we both lay side by side on the broken bottles and stones of the entry for several minutes, without a single word passing between us, without any physical contact.

I think by this time we were both crying, but I couldn't be sure.

12

That night was a turning point in my life. These were my closest friends. I felt I had had enough.

Shannon got a job in town, and this gave me the opportunity to see her more often, and get out of my street. We would sit in the central library at lunchtimes holding hands. Nobody we knew went there. Her mother made her cheese and tomato sandwiches, and we shared them. Sometimes I would go to the department store where she worked, and look at the cheap shirts and socks. I never bought anything. I had no money. I would flick through the T-shirts, and she would just smile over, but we couldn't really talk there. Some of the girls knew her, most of them lived up her way. All of them were of her own persuasion, as they say up our way. They were all called Marie, and Theresa and Roisin. It was that kind of shop. We had ours, they had theirs. It's the way things are.

Kingo's da sent for me a few weeks later. One of his friends came to fetch me from the park one afternoon, and he told me that there was nothing to worry about. Big Phil just wanted a wee word in my ear. So Philip King and I sat in an upstairs room of the club and he told me that he was pleased that I had co-operated with the hit team sent to discipline Hammerhead that night. He told me that my father would have been proud that I had put the Organization first before personal relationships. But I told him that I wasn't sure my father would have been particularly proud of me that night. I didn't elaborate.

Kingo's da explained to me that my actions made perfect sense in the end because it was the Organization, and only the Organization, that could guarantee our future, our wee tenuous hold on the land of our fathers.

'Your friends are important, but what can they guarantee you?' he said. 'And besides it all worked out well with Hammerhead in the end, he just needed a wee fright.'

I sat there in that dark room reflecting on what he had to say. Light filtered in from the street. The blinds were half down, I didn't know why. 'Security' is all they ever said. I noticed that Kingo's da had a little jagged scar just below his left eye. It looked as if he had been cut by glass. I had never noticed it before. I sat there wondering whether this had been done on active service or in some bar-room brawl. I think I knew which it was.

'We need somebody to look after our interests,' continued Big Phil. 'That's why we have to put the Organization first. Paisley's only out for number one. He spends too much of his time at Westminster or Strasbourg rather than talking to grassroots Protestants. The loyalist paramilitaries need to spend more time developing a coherent political agenda, like Sinn Fein, starting at grassroots levels on local councils and upwards. The paramilitaries have got to get their act together politically. But when they do, we're going to be a powerful force. Powerful. That's why we have to support them in any way we can.'

I listened to everything he had to say, and then went away and thought about it some more, not in the abstract, but in the concrete, up that entry with Hammerhead lying there with the loose chippings stuck in his back. When I thought of Hammerhead's pock-marked back, and the hit man going on about Hammerhead filling his pants, it all seemed different somehow.

The lads from the corner knew I was serious about somebody, so I had to make a whole history for the girl from the

Antrim Road that I was supposed to be seeing. Shannon helped me out. We sat in the library and gave her a name and, of course, an appropriate date of birth. She was Sagittarian like Shannon herself. We made up her hair colour, and her style of clothes, we even got down to sexual preference. That's what the lads at the corner really wanted to hear about, what nice middle-class girls with fresh soft make-up are really like when they're on their own with you, up some entry, with your hand down their knickers.

Billy was back at the corner. He never talked about his ex-wife. Sometimes I was worried that he might be able to see some of her in the persona that Shannon and I had constructed for my imaginary girlfriend, but he never did. Perhaps there was none of Shannon in her, except the star sign. He slipped back into life there with great ease, as if he had never been away.

Hammerhead was never the same again with me, even after I swore to him on my father's grave that I knew all along that it was all just a charade that night up the entry, that it was all just one big act. But he never believed me. He said he could tell by my face that this wasn't the case, and he would never forget that expression of mine. He told me my face that night was burnt into his memory, like a branding iron on a cow's arse. I told him memory wasn't like that.

He just said I had shopped him, and that he knew I'd shopped him, and I knew I'd shopped him, so there was no point in talking about it any further.

Tucker wasn't at the corner so much. All he ever said was that he was busy. And when he did come down he was always acting the big man. Some of the lads wanted to get close to him because of who he knew. I thought he was standing in judgement on the rest of us. We all watched our behaviour in front of him, and we watched what we said. It just wasn't the same somehow. It can't be the same when you're being that careful, when you're watching what you say and what you do.

Shannon took me into a chapel one Saturday afternoon. I had never been in a Roman Catholic church before. We don't even call them churches, we call them chapels. We sat there in this most forbidden of all places, looking at the deep colours of crimson and gold lit by candles sitting on tin foil. I studied Jesus on the cross with the blood in his ankles and in the palms of his hands. A deep red blood. Up in our church the cross was empty, there was no blood anywhere. All the suffering was already done, or it was still waiting for us. She showed me how she crossed herself, and she got me to kiss her on the lips at the back of the chapel. She asked me if I thought the Troubles would ever end. I told her I didn't think so because there were too many people whose lives depended on them going on for ever.

'What would they do?' I asked. 'What would they do with themselves?'

She told me that this was a very cynical point of view. And then pointing around the dark empty chapel asked, 'Is this what it's all about then? Is it anything to do with religion at all?'

I looked over at the candles and the gold braid climbing up the bit at the side of the altar and the blood seeping out of Jesus's fresh wounds and Jesus pointing at his heart which looked like a squashed apricot and the gold angels with their gold trumpets, and I said, 'I don't think so. I don't think it's got anything to do with this as such.'

I said I had read somewhere recently that Gerry Adams wanted all the IRA prisoners out of English jails and back in Northern Ireland. After that, I said, 'If ever there was a ceasefire they'd be asking for an amnesty for all the IRA men. They'd be opening the gates and letting all these cowboys walk free. Then when they got out, they'd be riding the range naturally. The fellas in the big picture.

'But what are they going to be doing when they're back on the streets?' I asked Shannon. 'What kind of work will they get? They'll have to do something. What have they been trained for except killing people? Perhaps Gerry Adams will get them all jobs. He used to be a barman. Perhaps he'll get them all fixed up in bars all over Belfast.'

She told me that I was the worst cynic she had ever met, that once the politics were sorted out then everything else would follow. Everything else would just slot into place. I told her she had her head in the clouds.

At nights we would meet in town, in a neutral bar, half-way between the Shankill and the Falls, sprinkled with people like us, people who didn't really belong or didn't really care. But if the truth be known there were fewer from the latter category. And we would make one drink last a whole evening.

One night this old grey-haired man sat down beside us. We were sitting beside each other on a long seat, and he just backed himself into the seat on the other side of Shannon without saying anything. He had nicotine-stained fingers. I noticed these because his cigarette had burnt right down, and he was still trying to smoke it. He was drinking Black Bush and water, the water from a white jug with a picture of Dunluce Castle on the side. He liked topping the Black Bush up as he drank it. Every time he called the waitress over he gave us a wink. I knew he would talk sooner or later. We sat in a little huddle; I had my arm around her shoulder, keeping him out. Then a different waitress put some ice in his glass.

'No ice,' he said. 'You don't put ice in Black Bush. Don't you know nothing around here?'

He looked at me, and I knew that I would have to answer him if he spoke to me. 'She put ice in my Black Bush,' he said.

'Terrible,' I said, without really knowing why.

'Would you put ice in your Black Bush?' he asked.

'No, I don't think I would,' I said.

'Would your wife there?' he said.

'No, she wouldn't either. But she's not my wife, she's my girlfriend,' I said.

He then started to serenade us with 'Hello, Young Lovers, Wherever You Are'. He told us that he had just got out of hospital, and that they had told him they could do no more for him. He had cancer. He was celebrating being alive. So he had come to town to numb his senses. He bought us a drink, and shook Shannon's hand. He held on to it for a long time, and I watched those long brown fingers hold her delicate white hand, and I felt jealous. As ridiculous as that was, I felt sexually jealous that some other man was touching her. Even this old man stained brown on the outside and eaten with cancer inside. I wanted him to release her. I didn't want him to touch her at all. I felt slightly ashamed of my emotions that night, just as I felt ashamed every time I went to see her in the shop where she worked and felt a pang of jealousy whenever some good-looking customer glanced across at her.

The old man told us that he was called Andy. He asked us our names. We didn't want to lie. Why should we in a bar like that? That's why we were there – to be ourselves. Shannon told him her first name, and he said, 'What kind of name is that?' I knew from his look that he knew. 'Are you from the Free State?' he asked. We knew what he was saying. He was telling us that he knew she was a Taig and I was a confused little Prod out drinking in no man's land because we didn't want anybody to see us together. He touched her arm, and told us that Belfast was a very small-minded little town, and that we shouldn't worry about it. He bought us another drink. Three Black Bush, no ice, and he poured the water from the jug for us.

'Holy water,' he said. 'This is holy water – what makes Ireland great.' But I didn't know whether he was talking about the water or the whiskey. He clinked glasses with us. I went to the toilet, and when I got back I could hear Shannon screaming at him. She was crying. She told me that as soon as I had left the table he had said he wanted to show Shannon his fat finger with no nail. I didn't understand it at first, but she did. She was calling him a 'fucking dirty old man'. He didn't even finish his drink. He called her a 'wee Fenian bitch' as he was gathering his coat up and a 'wee Fenian whore'. He said he didn't know what I was doing with her.

'Just listen to her,' he said. 'Listen to that fucking language. Just listen to how she's talking to an old man and me with cancer as well.'

He seemed to be implying that a nice Presbyterian girl would have just sat there soaking up his barely concealed indecency in the smoky half-light of that bar.

We stayed in the bar until it closed and then I walked her to Castle Street and she got one of her black taxis and then I made my way through Smithfield to get one of mine. Our sectarian taxis institutionalized our divisions. There was always the risk that one or other of us would be recognized, but I wouldn't let her go for a taxi on her own. I was too possessive for that.

We never went to clubs any more because we couldn't afford it. But then one night, quite out of the blue, she told me that she really wanted to go back to the club that we'd been to on our first date, 'for old times' sake'. She said she would pay for the drinks. She was in a restless mood, as agitated as I had ever seen her. When I asked her what was wrong, she just said she was worried about her brother. He had been getting very depressed lately. She seemed distant the whole evening, and when I went to the toilet I came back to find some Englishman chatting to her. I saw him trying to give her his telephone number. I was surprised it had got that far in that short time. But then again, my mother always says that the English are a very forward people. We had an argument about it. She thought I was accusing her of 'whoring around'. I wasn't. These were words I didn't even know, and if you don't know the words, how can you accuse somebody of it? I was just jealous, that was all.

Then she said she wanted to leave early. She said she would get one of the unlicensed taxis because I was too soft to hail a proper one. I hardly saw the driver, but I think it was the same driver as last time. I recognized the ginger hair. Hammerhead and this man were the only two people I knew with hair that colour. It's funny being able to pin-point somebody from a tuft of hair. She didn't give me a backward glance, as the taxi did a U-turn in the street and accelerated away towards West Belfast, and the murals of the PLO and Nelson Mandela and the republican struggle that they were always trying to make legitimate with their images of victimhood and suffering, and I was left there on the street, alone and angry.

I had arranged to meet her the following lunchtime in the library. She was half an hour late. I could hear my stomach rumbling, that's how late she was. Then I saw her coming in and I knew immediately that something was terribly wrong. She was covering herself, that's the only way that I can describe it, she was covering herself up from everybody. She was covering herself up from the world. She was walking with her long coat wrapped around her, clinging on to it like a blanket. When she sat down and pulled the coat back, I knew what was wrong. She almost didn't have to tell me. I just knew it. I sensed it, if you like. We were that close I could sense things from her. I asked her what was wrong, but she didn't answer. She just sat there sniffing, the tears running down her face. She stemmed the tears just below her cheekbones, brushing them sideways, until her whole face glistened with tear and snatter. Like a child with red cheeks glistening from all that crying.

I looked at her and I knew from her eyes, from the tears. 'I've been raped,' she said eventually.

She said it quietly, as if in shame, like you might in confession in chapel. I've never witnessed a confession, but I imagine that's how it sounds. You say it in a low voice as if you are genuinely sorry. 'Bless me, Father, for I have sinned.' She had instructed me a little bit in what Catholics do. I knew how they started the confession. We sat there in silence in this vast tomb of a room, with old men and women hunched over books, reading about Irish history steeped in human tragedy and suffering, oblivious to this very human suffering happening right in front of them. I felt physically sick.

'Who did it?' I asked, after a long dark pause.

She wouldn't look at me. I could feel her fingers stroking the back of my hand, as if to say that she knew that it would be difficult for me too. Her fingers rubbed the same spot on my hand again and again, irritating me rather than consoling me, adding to my anger rather than dampening it down.

'Who did it?' I asked again. This time after a shorter pause, my irritation showing.

'It was that taxi driver. He kept looking at me. He pulled in on the way home. He was carrying a knife.'

'Did you put up a fight?'

I just asked this without thinking. I didn't mean to say it. I wasn't even thinking it. I just asked this, as if I thought this is what you are supposed to say in the circumstances. It was like a natural reaction. Or rather like how a policeman or a priest might naturally react. She looked angry at me. I couldn't blame her, to be honest.

'He had a fucking knife. Didn't you hear what I've just told you? He would have used it. There was nothing I could do. He had a fucking big knife in his hand.'

I squeezed her hand, so hard that I could see her knuckles

turning white. I squeezed until she said more, at least that's how it felt at the time.

'I know him as well,' she said. 'That's the ridiculous thing. I know him. I can't go to the police though. He's in something up our way. He's a Provisional or something. He'd have me wiped out. I even know his name, and where he lives. I pass his house all the time. I see him and his wife and his two wee ones. I know the cunt.'

I felt angrier than I had ever done in my life. I felt angry at her, and I felt angry at him. I wanted to kill him. I couldn't bear the thought of what he had done. I couldn't bear the thought of him being inside her. Perhaps things had been building up inside me; it was as if all of my anger and guilt over Hammerhead and Tucker, and the unresolved guilt and anguish about my father, was suddenly finding a productive outlet. Perhaps it was just love, love can make you possessive like that, love can make you angry too. I knew that inside.

But I also knew in that instant that I would do something. It was like a torrent raging down the side of a hill, sweeping aside anything that stood in its way. I felt myself being carried away by the anger. I asked her for his name. I was sure she could feel the rage within me, so I was surprised, shocked even, when she told me his name and gave me his address immediately without hesitation, without asking me not to do anything stupid. Like people do in these situations. She just said, 'Be careful.' That's all. 'Be careful.' I walked her to the bus stop in the stoniest of silences, and left her there. I looked back and saw this small vulnerable person huddled up in her big winter coat. She looked how she had done that first day in the park, and I felt this rage within me.

I went home and sat in my room and cried. Then I went to see Tucker at his house. I went with a story about an IRA man who had threatened me. Shannon was never mentioned. It was a story about a chance encounter with an old man just out of hospital, a man suffering from stomach cancer, and this yahoo, this hood from the IRA threatening him with a gun just to show what a big man he really was because the old man had spilt his drink. In the story I intervened and he threatened to blow me away along with all the other fucking loyalist cowards from North Belfast. Tucker sat there, taking it all in. Then he spoke.

'It's a pity I wasn't there with you,' he said. 'We could have got the gun off him and given him a good kicking. It's a pity we don't know where this hood lives or we could give him a nasty surprise.'

'But the funny thing is that I do know where he lives,' I said. 'The old man knew him, you see.'

Tucker looked at me with a slightly quizzical expression on his face. 'How did he know him? Were they friends? Was this a wee dispute between friends out for a drink?'

'No, they weren't friends,' I said. 'They used to be neighbours.'

'Do you mean that this old man with cancer lives up in West Belfast?' asked Tucker. 'Do you mean to say that he's a Taig as well?'

'No, what I mean to say is that he used to be a neighbour years ago,' I said, 'at the start of the Troubles, but he was put out of his house along with all the other Protestants from up there. They were all burnt out.'

'Oh,' said Tucker. 'But how do you know that your man is in the Provisionals?'

'The old man knew,' I said. 'He told me.'

'Then we better have a word with the old man,' said Tucker.

'But I didn't get his address,' I said. 'That's the one thing that I didn't get.'

Tucker looked at me as if to say this was an odd tale. He knew that there was something not quite right about it. But he couldn't put his finger on it. He also knew that I was not the kind of person who fingered people for no good reason, so on that basis and on that basis alone he said that he would take me to see Big Phil for me to talk to him about it.

Tucker rang him, and I could hear him giving Kingo's da the gist of our conversation. Tucker walked me to a house that I didn't know, a newer house than ours about a mile away, on a new estate. I don't know who it belonged to. Big Phil sat there with three others. He told me to calm down, and that reckless action was dangerous action. He asked me to tell him exactly what had happened. He paced up and down the living room as he listened. I told him my story, which had improved from the first telling, the way that stories do.

He sat back down again. 'My first question is, What were you doing in this bar?' asked Big Phil. 'Why were you drinking there?'

I told him all about the girl from my school, the Sagittarian from the Antrim Road who preferred drinking in town.

'But what was the IRA man doing drinking there?' he asked. 'Surely he'd have a better night out in one of his own regular haunts. And what was he doing tooled up? That doesn't make any sense. What was he thinking about going into town carrying like that?'

I said that I had no idea, that the minds of republican hit men were beyond me.

'What was his name again?' asked Big Phil. I told him. The name seemed to ring a bell. 'Do we have any intelligence on this man?' he asked. He addressed this question to the three other men in the room. One nodded.

'I know him,' he said. 'He's in the IRA all right. He's a right cunt as well. I've heard that he was involved in that shooting up by the lough shore last summer.'

'Bingo,' said Big Phil.

For two days I sat at home in front of the television that still didn't work with anger churning my stomach over, distracting me, pulling my thoughts this way and that. Even my mother kept out of my way. I saw Tucker getting into a car late one night, and didn't really think anything of it, even when I saw a car following his out of the street. I didn't realize that this was the hit.

It was on the news the following day, the local news that is. A taxi driver suspected of being in the Provisional IRA was shot dead by loyalist assassins on his way to his taxi depot. He used this depot, against the rules, for his car which was unlicensed. The news story managed to sneak this in, so that we would all know what kind of man he really was. One of the loyalists was shot and wounded in the attack. He later died of his wounds in hospital. They didn't say his name.

I found out later that this was Tucker's first operation, and his last. Hammerhead and I both went to the funeral, along with Big Phil and most of the neighbourhood. I tried contacting Shannon at her sister's on the day of the funeral but she wasn't there. I was desperate to talk to her. Her sister said that she hadn't seen her for a while, and had heard that she wasn't very well.

Tucker didn't get a military funeral, because his mother said she wanted something simple. So we buried him from our local church, where we used to sit together with our heads in our hands, leaning forward and talking when we were supposed to be praying. I read the lesson in church, because I was the educated one. Big Phil told me not to feel bad. I didn't make Tucker do it. He was a soldier. This taxi driver was the enemy. It was as simple as that. There had been other intelligence on this man. My wee bit of intelligence was just the icing on the cake. These were Kingo's da's words, not mine. Nobody could remember the taxi driver's name any longer. Not even me. It was Sean something. That's all I remember. Sean something. His second name was hard to pronounce and therefore hard to remember.

But as I lay in bed the night of Tucker's funeral, and I

213

thought about my duplicity and lies brought about by my rage at what had happened to Shannon, I could feel the guilt eating right through me, like a worm in my soul. I thought of Tucker being laid to rest in that wet, heaving mud up at Roselawn and my heart shuddered. But I was glad that the man with the goatee beard, the man I had hardly even seen, had been killed for what he had done to Shannon and to me. I was responsible for murder, but I was glad.

I needed to talk to Shannon, but I couldn't contact her. Eventually, I walked up to her house, and there her mother told me that she and her brother and the child had gone over to England to somewhere in Birmingham to get a break from Belfast, and its sectarian murder. She told me that Shannon had said she didn't want me to contact her. She wanted a clean break. She told her mother she had had enough of Belfast. Her mother wouldn't even tell me which part of Birmingham she had moved to, in case I tried to follow her over. The mother also added that she knew I wasn't Mary O'Neill's son, and that her daughter had had quite enough of liars.

A month later, it snowed. It was unusual for Belfast to have snow so early in the winter, for the snow to get across the Irish Sea, but I was pleased to see the grey streets covered for once in a white, crisp purity. I was feeling melancholy so I went to the corner by myself and stood there quite alone, listening to the muffled noises of feet breaking through layers of crisp snow as people trudged home from work. It was there that I saw Billy come walking along. I hadn't really spoken to him since that day in the park when I first saw Shannon.

Rubber Man saw me and nodded, and came up and stood beside me. 'What a fucking carry-on,' he said. 'Poor old fucking Tucker.'

We stood there in silence, we could almost have been paying our respects.

It was Billy who mentioned Shannon. I would never have brought the subject up.

'Do you remember that wee girl I was with that day up by the Wendy hut?' he asked. 'The wee girl I married?'

I nodded.

'She was a Taig, did you know that?'

I said I didn't. 'How would I have known? You can't tell, you know, not by looking anyway,' I said.

'Do you not think so?' he said. 'I think you can,' he said, 'but that's just my personal opinion. I've no excuses about marrying her. I guessed that she was a Taig when I met her, and that's what she turned out to be. I'm always right when it comes to that sort of thing.'

I nodded quietly. I didn't like Billy talking about her. I didn't like the thought of the two of them having sex together, even though he was before me, so to speak. I tried to think about something else, but every time I tried to focus my mind, I just saw this little dark image of Tucker with his funny little walk coming down our street, and getting into the back of a car. A wee bit vulnerable, like my da.

'We split up a while ago. Did you know that?' he said.

'No,' I said.

'Do you know why?' he asked.

I thought of Shannon's bruises that day on the beach, but that all now seemed so long ago, with all that had happened in the mean time.

'No,' I said.

'Because she was a fucking headcase. That's why. She has this brother who was big in the drugs scene in Belfast. The IRA got fed up with the guy and gave him a double knee job. That's how serious a fucking dealer he was. Anyway, your woman knows the names of the guys who carried out the shooting, because her brother recognized them. She doesn't tell me any of this though. The next thing is she tells me this guy raped her at a party. She thought I was

215

going to use my contacts up our way to have your man blown away. She must have thought I was fucking daft.'

I said, 'What?' before I realized what I had said. I stood there shivering, waiting for Billy to tell me more. The cold seemed to be conducted through the soles of my feet and was creeping up through my whole body.

'I made some enquiries about this party that she went to with her sister, she said,' said Billy. 'She didn't realize that I knew a few people who had been to the party. It was mixed, you see. Your man, who she said had raped her, wasn't even there. She must have thought I was a right mug. You see she couldn't get anybody up her own way to do it, so she thought she'd get me to set it up for her.'

I stood there listening to this, and I could not swallow. My throat had gone as dry as dead bone. I felt as if I was going to choke to death.

'I think that's the only reason she married me,' said Billy, 'to get me to do her dirty work for her. She was a scheming little bitch. When I found out, I went berserk and gave her a smack in the mouth. She took the kid and fucked off, but I haven't seen her since. And do you want to know something?' asked Billy.

'What?' I said.

'I don't fucking want to see either of them again. People like that can get you into a lot of trouble in this little town of ours. Good fucking riddance to the pair of them, that's what I say.'

'Fucking hell,' I said. This came out full of anguish, but Billy didn't hear it.

'Exactly,' said Billy. 'Fucking hell.'

He made a low sighing noise, like wind rushing out of a tunnel, the last breath of a man perhaps, a final comment on life and all its twists and turns and ups and downs.

'Good fucking riddance,' he said again.

'Good fucking riddance,' came the echo from within me,

but the emotion inside choked my breath and silenced my voice and made this little assertion of solidarity completely inaudible to anybody but me. Only I could hear this breathless inner voice as I stood there numb in that snow, with my memories ticking away inside reminding me of my every word and my every action that led step by step to the death of my closest and most valued friend.

I knew then that my memories were going to be savage and remorseless bedfellows for the rest of my life.

And I still know it now, a year and a bit on. I swallowed my pride and hardened my sensitivities and went back to school, and smiled when I had to, and wore plain grey socks and said that I preferred these socks to almost anything else. And everybody at school, both staff and pupils, told me that I had matured immeasurably in the time I had been away, that the break had helped me grow. I wasn't so difficult any more. But it was easy really, compared to everything else I knew.

And here I sit in a ceasefire in Belfast, preparing to go to university in England. Everything has changed now in this city of ours. The *Belfast Telegraph* is predicting in its diary column that the demilitarized look could be the new big trend this autumn in Northern Ireland. Security staff at the Bass-owned Ulster Brewery on the Glen Road have been issued with new uniforms – snappy navy blazers, grey trousers, white shirts and company ties replacing the old military-style brown tunics, trousers and peaked caps. Soldiers on the streets have dumped their hard hats, Belfast is becoming demilitarized, as the IRA always wanted. That's what my mother says.

But Kingo's da is still around, he's still making himself busy, still poking his nose into things, still making a little bit of cash, and still not really working. And he's keeping his eye out, which is just as well, according to a lot of people

217

around here. And my mother still works up in the mill that doesn't really make anything, and she still earns less than the machine operators, and she still can't get invited to the club on a Saturday night because she's nobody really.

I sit here thinking about Shannon a lot. It was love, I know that now, it wasn't just lust or sexual jealousy or any of those sorts of things. It was love and it hasn't faded and I think that one day I might even bump into her across the water, and we can talk about all that happened. She might be able to explain it all to me from her point of view so that I can try to come to terms with it. Then I might understand. I long for that day when I see her, and we sit down together on some park bench somewhere in England, and she holds my hand and she tells me what she remembers about it all, and I can see the whole picture differently.

But the funny thing is that I've already started to forget how she sounded. That voice of hers is fading already. I hear other girls' voices in town, girls from up the Falls and from Poleglass and Twinbrook with that same twang, which is a little bit different from ours, and I think they all sound like her. I can't keep hers separate any more in my head from all the others. The voices of all the Maries and the Roisins and the Theresas and Shannon are all somehow becoming one. Kingo's da was never right. Our memory isn't here to protect us, it's here to torment us. I want to cling on to that sound of her, and hear how she talked to me, but I can't.

And one day no doubt without her voice in my head I'll forget what she said as well. It's just my words that I'll remember, and what lies I told Tucker and Kingo's da and everybody else from my street and the next. And without Shannon's voice, I'll just be able to remember half the story about the rape and the taxi driver and Tucker and all the events that led to him ending up in Roselawn not far from my father, where the wind whips across those muddy fields knocking the flowers over out of their vases and where the red, white and blue petals get trampled into the wet dirty soil, and nobody really notices from one week to the next. Half the story that led to all of this.

I pack my bags to leave Belfast for a new life, with this one damning thought somewhere at the back of my mind. I know that one day, and the day probably is not that far off, I'll be sitting alone across the water thinking about my past and what friendship can mean and remembering our fallen comrade, as Kingo's da always calls him, and I'll just be able to conjure up *my* words and *my* lies as if they alone were responsible for everything that happened. And I know already that the guilt, which will come from this partial and flawed memory, will make my life almost unbearable.

HEAD TO HEAD

Geoffrey Beattie

In his two BBC Radio 5 Live series of *Head to Head*, psychologist and writer Geoffrey Beattie proved himself a master interviewer.

Time and again his gentle but incisive probing threw up extraordinary insights: that Naseem Hamed is incapable of feeling fear; that Chris Boardman hates cycling; that Liz McColgan considers herself fat when she sees herself running on TV; that Jonathan Edwards sees the work of the devil in everything, especially athletics.

Each broadcast interview lasted a mere 25 minutes, but was edited down from at least double that. The full content of those interviews, in print for the first time, provides a compelling window into the souls of these singular, driven men and women; the sort of people they are – and think they are; why they do what they do – and how; what it means to win – and lose.

The collection as a whole adds up to the most complete inquiry ever published into the psychology of our sporting heroes, and makes gripping reading for all sports fans.

£9.99   0 575 06358 0

A Gollancz
Paperback Original

ON THE ROPES

Geoffrey Beattie

Geoffrey Beattie spent two years training and hanging out with the boxers in Brendan Ingle's famous Sheffield gym, which has produced a string of boxing stars, including the world featherweight champion, Naseem Hamed.

Beattie watches the boxers training and sparring, listens as they tell him of their aspirations, and observes their special camaraderie. And he follows them at play in nightclubs and bars, and in their enjoyment of brutal, illicit sports like dog-fighting and bare-knuckle fighting.

'Beattie can write about the low life of boxing like no one else . . . [He] has got the smell of the gym in his lungs. He breathes resin, sweat and soiled towels. He even goes three rounds himself with Mick Mills . . . Not since I first went ringside with the late Ring Lardner have I so enjoyed a book on boxing'   Julian Critchley, *Daily Telegraph*

'One of the books of the year . . . Sharp, jabbing writing; hard, compassionate journalism'   Peter Whitebrook, *Scotland on Sunday*

'An authentic, skilful account of grit and graft in a tough northern city – a tale oozing perspiration, aspiration and, all too often, desperation'
          Andrew Shields, *Time Out*

£6.99   0 575 40076 5

INDIGO

BLEEDING LONDON

Geoff Nicholson

London is a character in Geoff Nicholson's supremely entertaining new novel, and the characters are London. London is a city of maps, and the sexual possibilities of maps. What would it feel like to walk down every street in the London *A-Z*? It is a city in which a visiting Sheffield stripper can be violently mistreated, and in which her vengeful boyfriend can conceal himself until the job is done. It is a city of obsessives, of insouciant sadists, of innocents. It is BLEEDING LONDON.

With this subtle, complex and darkly funny novel Geoff Nicholson joins the select ranks – Martin Amis, Peter Ackroyd, Iain Sinclair – of those writers who have anatomized London in these twentieth-century dog-days. BLEEDING LONDON is a triumph.

'As packed with strange and comic and menacing incidents and characters as any night-bus lurching round Trafalgar Square . . . Geoff Nicholson obviously boasts a rich and arcane knowledge of the city and exploits that to the full'   Harry Ritchie, *The Times*

'[Nicholson's] BLEEDING LONDON is a dark, frayed and filthy place . . . filled with weird sex, arbitrary violence and obscure threat. He produces comic lines when you least expect them, making you laugh out loud'   Geraldine Bedell, *New Statesman*

£5.99   0 575 40056 0

IND/GO